City of the Horizon

CITY OF THE HORIZON

Anton Gill

City of the Horizon

A Felony & Mayhem mystery

PRINTING HISTORY
First UK edition: 1991
Felony & Mayhem edition: 2005

ISBN: 1-933397-11-X

Manufactured in the United States of America

For M.H.L.

THE BACKGROUND TO HUY'S EGYPT

AUTHOR'S NOTE

The historical background to the story which follows is broadly correct, but the majority of the characters are fictional. We know a good deal about Ancient Egypt because its inhabitants were highly developed, literate, and had a sense of history; even so, experts estimate that in the 200 years since the science of Egyptology began, only twenty-five per cent of what could be known has been revealed, and there is still much disagreement about certain dates and events amongst scholars. However, I do apologise to Egyptologists and purists, who may read this and take exception to such unscholarly conduct, for the occasional freedoms I have allowed myself.

The nine years of the reign of the young Pharoah Tutankhamun, 1361–1352 B.C., were troubled ones for Egypt. They came at the end of the Eighteenth Dynasty, the most glorious of all the thirty dynasties of the Empire. Tutankhamun's predecessors had been mainly illustrious warrior kings, who created a new empire and consolidated the old; but just before him a strange, visionary pharaoh had occupied the throne: Akhenaten. He had thrown out all the old gods and replaced them with one, the Aten, who had his being in the life-giving sunlight. Akhenaten was the world's first recorded philosopher and the inventor of monotheism. In the seventeen years of his reign he made enormous changes in the way his country thought and was run; but in the process he lost the whole of the northern empire (modern Palestine and Syria), and brought the country to the brink of ruin. Now, powerful enemies were thronging on the northern and eastern frontiers.

Akhenaten's religious reforms had driven doubt into the minds of his people after generations of unchanged certainty which went back to before the building of the pyramids one thousand years earlier, and although the empire itself, already over 1,500 years old at the time of these stories, had been through bad times before, Egypt now entered a short dark age. Akhenaten had not been popular with the priest-administrators of the old religion, whose power he took away, or with ordinary people, who saw him as a defiler of their long-held beliefs, especially in the afterlife and the dead. Since his death in 1362 B.C., the new capital city he had built for himself (Akhetaten—the City of the Horizon), quickly fell into ruin as power reverted to Thebes (the Southern Capital; the northern seat of government was at Memphis). Akhenaten's name was cut from every monument, and people were not even allowed to speak it.

Akhenaten died without a direct heir, and the short reigns of the three kings who succeeded him, of which Tutankhamun's was the second and by far the longest, were fraught with uncertainty. During this time the pharaohs themselves had their power curbed and controlled by Horemheb, formerly Commander-in-Chief of Akhenaten's army, but now bent on fulfilling his own ambition to restore the empire and the old religion, and to become pharaoh himself—he did so finally in 1348 B.C. and reigned for twenty-eight years, the last king of the Eighteenth Dynasty, marrying Akhenaten's sister-in-law to reinforce his claim to the throne.

Egypt was to rally under Horemheb, and early in the Nineteenth Dynasty it achieved one last glorious peak under Rameses II. It was by far the most powerful and the wealthiest country in the known world, rich in gold, copper and precious stones. Trade was carried out the length of the Nile from the coast to Nubia, and on the Mediterranean (the Great Green), and the Red Sea as far as Punt (Somaliland). But it was a narrow strip of a country, clinging to the banks of the Nile and hemmed in to the east and west by deserts, and governed by three seasons: Spring, Shemu, was the time of drought, from February to May; Summer, Akhet, was the time of the Nile flood, from June to October; and Autumn, Peret, was the time of coming forth, when the crops grew. The Ancient Egyptians lived closer to the seasons than we do. They also believed that the heart was the centre of thought.

The decade in which the stories take place—a minute period of Ancient Egypt's 3,000-year history—was nevertheless a crucial one for the country. It was becoming aware of the world beyond its frontiers, and of the possibility that it, too, might one day be conquered and come to an end. It was a time of uncertainty, questioning, intrigue and violence. A distant mirror in which we can see something of ourselves.

The Ancient Egyptians worshipped a great number of gods. Some of them were restricted to cities or localities, while others waxed and waned in importance with time. Certain gods were duplications of the same 'idea.' Here are some of the most important, as they appear in the stories:

AMUN the chief god of the Southern Capital, Thebes. Represented as a man, and associated with the supreme sun god, Ra. Animals dedicated to him were the ram and the goose.

ANUBIS the jackal god of embalming.

ATEN the god of the sun's energy, represented as the sun's disk whose rays end in protecting hands.

BES a dwarf god, part lion. Protector of the hearth.

GEB the earth god, represented as a man.

HAPY the god of the Nile.

HATHOR the cow goddess; the suckler of the king.

HORUS the hawk god, son of Osiris and Isis, and therefore a member of the most important trinity in Ancient Egyptian theology.

ISIS the divine mother.

KHONS the god of the moon; son of Amun.

MAAT the goddess of truth.

MIN the god of human fertility.

MUT wife of Amun, originally a vulture goddess. The vulture was the animal of Upper (southern) Egypt. Lower (northern) Egypt was represented by the cobra.

OSIRIS the god of the underworld. The afterlife was of central importance to the thinking of the Ancient Egyptians.

RA the great god of the sun.

SET the god of storms and violence; brother and murderer of Osiris. Very roughly equivalent to Satan.

SOBEK the crocodile god.

THOTH the ibis-headed god of writing. His associated animal was the baboon.

PRINCIPAL CHARACTERS OF *CITY OF THE HORIZON*

(in order of appearance)

fictional characters are in capital letters,
historical ones in lower case.

Smenkhkare	Pharaoh, 1364–1361 B.C.
Ay	Father-in-law of Akhenaten
Nefertiti	Wife of Akhenaten
Akhenaten	Pharaoh, 1379–1362 B.C.
HUY	Scribe
Horemheb	Former Commander-in-Chief of Akhenaten's army
AAHMES	Huy's ex-wife
MAIHERPRI	Medjay warrant officer
Tutankhamun	Pharaoh, 1361–1352 B.C.
TEHUTY	Huy's ex-brother-in-law
AMOTJU	Owner of a shipping line; friend of Huy
MUTNEFERT	A girl from Mitanni. Amotju's mistress
REKHMIRE	A powerful priest-administrator
RAMOSE	Amotju's deceased father
ASET	Amotju's sister
Amenophis III	Pharaoh, 1417–1379 B.C.
ANI	Barge captain
TAHEB	Amotju's wife
INTEF	Medjay officer

City of the Horizon

CHAPTER 1

At the moment of his death darkness covered the land. The very sun at noon was blotted out by a black disc—sent there by Set, the demon, some said; and for an hour midnight reigned. Was it a sign that the sun mourned the pharaoh—or that the old gods approved his death?

King Smenkhkare could not have chosen a worse time to die. The scribe, Huy, thought that this might be his opinion more than anyone else's; these days people were so quickly covering up their association with Akhenaten, his worship of one god, the Aten, and his theories about peace and light and universal brotherhood, that you could see the dust rise on the banks of the River from the breath of their recantations. Even Ay, the old king's Master of Horse and the father of the Great Queen, Nefertiti, was giving voice to reservations about the Aten.

Now that Smenkhkare, Akhenaten's adopted son and last loyal follower in any position of real power, had died, Huy wondered how long even the caution would last. After all, the last twelve years had seen the loss of the entire northern part of the empire. In his short reign, Akhenaten, with what most people regarded as crazy religious ideals, had lost what his great-great-grandfather had won, smashing the audacious power of Upper Retennu with the newly-found weapons of war: the chariot, the two-wood longbow, and spears of bronze, harder and more durable than copper. The messages had come in over a whole decade to the pharaoh, the God on Earth, the Unquestionable Power, to say that he was being questioned, challenged, destroyed in his might to the north. But the king had not sent a single reply to the torrent of requests for aid from his despairing vassals and governors.

Huy was not the only one to have been shattered by doubt at the speed with which the Aten had fallen. The Aten had been a fresh wind; the sweeping away, in ten hectic and cruel years, of two millennia of ever more hidebound and corrupt thinking, in a world where priestly ritual clogged the wheels of a government grown stale in the thirty decadent years of peace which preceded the young iconoclast's ascent to the Seat of God. But at the beginning there had been plenty of young men and women who were caught up in the New Thinking; the Black Land was at the height of its power, it stood at the apex of the world, ruled to the edge of the Great Green in the north, and beyond; ruled deep into the Red Land to the west, to the gold mines which lay between the River and the Eastern Sea, even south to the beginnings of the forest which those explorers who returned told of.

It was time to draw breath, to question. People had jumped at the chance to sweep away that jungle of old gods, that mess of superstition, raddled with the main-chancing of the priests of Amun. Huy allowed himself a wry smile as he recalled the joy with which they had set off north from the Southern Capital to people the New City, the City of the Horizon, itself a fresh skin after the old had been sloughed off.

How long ago had that been? Huy actually laughed now. Six years. To build a dam against two thousand years of entrenched thinking with only six years and a new town. What could they have been thinking of? The great mass of the people, backs bowed, still, whenever the pharaoh passed so that they would not see his face—Akhenaten's reforms hadn't stretched that far—had not been affected by so much as the whisper of a passing thought. It had been a revolution for the elite by the elite and as the old pharaoh's obsession had borne him into madness, it had all but cost the Black Land her supremacy.

And now Smenkhkare, the pharaoh, the God on Earth sustaining the Power of the Aten, the Disc of the Life-Giving Sun, was gone, aged twenty, having survived his mentor by six months. He had not carried the baton far alone.

How young they died, Huy thought. Akhenaten had been only nine years older, but then, his body had been wasted from birth, subject too, as if that was not enough, to those fits of holy ecstasy which threw his fragile frame on to the baked earth with the accurate violence of a professional wrestler, pinning him there and shaking him with such fury that his mouth foamed. Huy had seen it happen once. The king would have bitten through his tongue and broken his attenuated limbs by mere force of pressure, had there not been someone to prevent it. No one as lowly as Huy dared to begin to place an interpretation on the groans and frantic gurgling with which the god spoke through the king on those occasions, and their sense was never communicated to junior officials.

The king had died in such a fit, his soul soaring wherever it was it went, spiralling upwards towards his special god. A lonely fate; but Huy had wanted to believe in it too. Better towards the sun than remaining below in a tomb, however sumptuous, however plentifully stocked with magical food and servants of clay, however well protected by the spells of *The Book of the Dead*. Huy had wanted to believe, but hadn't come far enough along the road, hadn't been able to rid himself of the safe certainties of his fathers' fathers; but, seeing their tombs neglected by their successors, he now found himself believing only in life; what came before and after was a void his heart couldn't bring itself to contemplate.

Smenkhkare had died in his sleep; no one knew why. He had been a healthy young man, a keen hunter and a fond husband, though not yet a father. Only old Ay and the general, Horemheb, had visited the body before it was handed over to the embalmers.

The king hadn't held on to the reins of power well. The desert pirates of the north had approached dangerously close to the Delta, where the River entered the Great Green, and still the army merely patrolled and manoeuvred, never striking. At the same time, building work at the City of the Horizon ground to a halt. Ever since the death of Akhenaten, a trickle of people had started moving away. The place was on high ground above the River, but also in desert, unfriendly, baking in the season of Drought and plagued with mosquitoes in the seasons of Inundation and Coming Forth. Half-built, thrown up, with middens where there should have been drains, it seemed to Huy like a flower which had been blasted by a night frost in the act of opening. The life had gone out of it with the death of the old king; and although in parts of the city to the north, where the palaces reared among piles of builders' rubble like great sea-barges drawn on to the shore for repair, work was still going on in a half-hearted way, already in the suburbs the cheaper dwellings were beginning to crumble.

People needed to be told what to do, and instead, the king had died; it seemed as if he had run away. Then there had been the eclipse; and it had all happened in the middle of Peret, the season of Coming Forth, when the River's flood subsided, leaving the fields rich with the black silt which gave the land its name, but demanding every man's strength to work, clearing the irrigation canals and planting, as earth was reborn of water. It would be seventy days before the embalmers' work was complete, but the pharaoh's tomb was nowhere near finished. Many men badly needed on the land now would nevertheless be drafted to quarry and excavate and hew and haul limestone from the rock-face to bring the dwelling-place of the dead into at least a semblance of order. The dead were not usually vengeful; but the anger of a king beyond the grave was something to be avoided.

Huy, as he watched the elaborate rites and preparations taking place, wondered after all whether it wasn't the living who were more to be feared. He had already seen several of his senior colleagues—great scribes in their late thirties and forties—sent on missions to Nubia and to the gold mines of the eastern desert. These jobs were well beneath them, but even before the death of the old king it had become clear that their positions were no longer as secure as they had been when the glory of the Aten was at its height. Under Smenkhkare, power had shifted more and more to the general, Horemheb, and to Ay. Both had been loyal supporters of Akhenaten too, in the beginning. Perhaps it was just that they had been the first to see that the future did not, after all, lie with him.

None of the senior scribes had returned from their missions. Huy, at twenty-nine just emerging from a long and arduous apprenticeship, was beginning to wonder if the investment of time was going to be worth it. As he trudged down the narrow street of mud-packed earth that led to his house he looked back regretfully on his little achievements. His house, for one thing. It was one in a straggling row of identical dwellings for junior officials, each of mud-brick, with a small courtyard, a room downstairs and a room upstairs. He had lived here since his divorce three years earlier. He still found himself missing Aahmes, the child even more. They had long since returned to the Delta, and he didn't see them, though at least through his friends among the official couriers he was able to keep in irregular touch by letter.

His career had been a foregone conclusion, following in the footsteps of his father, Heby, a chief scribe in the court of Amenophis III in the Southern Capital. From the age of nine, Huy had known little other than study, learning the Three Scripts, and, interspersed with beatings ('a boy's ears are on his back'), the other subjects essential to a civil service career: arithmetic, drawing, bookkeeping, geometry, surveying, and even basic engineering. It had been a long haul. Now he hoped that it had not all been for nothing. He had ignored his more cautious father's warnings—Heby had sat on the fence until his death—and thrown in his lot with Akhenaten. He had come to the City of the Horizon without a second thought, imbued with the kind of pioneering spirit Akhenaten liked to see about him. Now the dust in the neglected and unsprinkled road seemed to him like the dust of that spirit.

The heat filled the street like folded linen. This physical presence sometimes made Huy long for the lands to the north, from where the blessed wind came. The couriers who had been there told him of the inexpressible green plain of the sea, which Huy had never seen and couldn't imagine. Escaping from the depressing thoughts which contemplation of his immediate future brought him, he embarked on a fantasy in which he patched things up with Aahmes and became the captain of one of the great Byblos ships which traded along the coastline and came down as far as the Northern Capital, whence their goods were transferred to high-prowed barges for the journey further upriver.

His reverie made him oblivious of the emptiness of the street, though the Matet-boat of the sun was almost at its height and the place should have been busy with people returning to eat and doze away the afternoon before work resumed. He broke out of it just as he turned the last corner before his house, and became aware at once both of his isolation, and of the man leaning against the already blistered acacia wood of his doorframe. He recognised what the man was immediately, and for a moment wondered if his approach had already been noticed, or if there was still a chance to duck away and hide. But the man was staring at Huy in the studiously bored, detached way policemen have when they have unpleasant news to impart. In any case, all along the blank walls of the meandering street there wasn't so much as an alley to dive down. And why fight fate? The sun shone and the River flowed. What more was there, in the end?

The policeman—a Medjay—was tall, taller than Huy, who was short and heavily built. He took advantage of his height as he lazily detached himself from the doorjamb on Huy's approach. But here was none of the deference a Medjay ought to show a court scribe. The Medjays had originally been recruited from a Nubian tribe who were skilled scouts, and who'd given the force their name. Now, the police came from all sections of society. This officer had the bony angularity, dark skin and flat features of someone from the far south—perhaps from Napata. His face was familiar to Huy but he could not place it. He wore a simple tan linen kilt. His long limbs shimmered in the heat. At his waist was a copper sword in a palm-leaf scabbard. Not a high-ranker then, thought Huy. But his presence explained the emptiness of the street. In the short months since Smenkhkare's death, with most of the people too busy in the fields to notice or care, General Horemheb had been busy. As the trickle of people away from the City of the Horizon increased, so did rumours of the renewed power of the priest-administrators in the Southern Capital. It was permitted again to speak the names of the old gods aloud. Those who had been close to Akhenaten were burying that fact if they could.

'Huy?'

'Yes.' There was no point in denying it, and no point in drawing attention to the omitted courtesy of his title, Court Scribe.

'Maiherpri, Warrant Officer.' Reminding Huy of his name. Looking at him with shy familiarity for a moment, and then his face closing in disappointment as Huy failed to register.

Why was the face familiar? Did it matter?

'Do you want to talk here, or inside?' continued the Medjay.

'You could have waited inside.'

'Not without permission.'

That, at least, was something. Huy glanced up the dusty street again. Some way distant, the now deserted Royal Palace towered, like a building in a dream.

Huy unlatched his door and went into the little courtyard. Following him, Maiherpri looked around. He saw a neat square, open to the sky but partially shaded by a tired vine.

'You live here alone?'

'Yes.' Since his divorce, there had not even been a house-servant. Hapu had gone with Aahmes; there was no room here even for a Syrian slave-girl.

It was customary to offer some form of refreshment, even to someone on an official visit. Maiherpri stood, obviously waiting.

'Some beer? Some bread?' asked Huy, and pointed to a low stool in the shade.

The policeman sat down, stiffly. He had been waiting in the sun for a long time; but despite his relief he would not unbend. He was a young man, on his dignity, conscious of being unwelcome, delaying his news to give it more importance. Now he wondered if the action of sitting hadn't robbed him of some advantage.

'First, there is the news of the God King's successor.'

'They had not wasted time, then,' thought Huy. Like his predecessor, Smenkhkare had died childless; but he had been an obvious favourite of Akhenaten's and married the eldest princess even before he had become co-regent. The bond had been sealed when Akhenaten himself had ceremonially married his oldest daughter too; but Smenkhkare had had no favourite or named successor. He had been young, and thought that there would be time enough to consider such things. Huy's heart delved quickly among the possibilities. There were two obvious contenders. But would they dare declare themselves so quickly?

'It is Tutankhaten.' Smenkhkare's half-brother. But Tutankhaten was only nine years old; there would have to be a regency.

The Medjay showed no sign of moving. There was more to come. So far there had been little to justify the expression on his face. Now, from a fold of his kilt, he produced a papyrus scroll, standing to hand it to the scribe. Huy paused for a moment before taking it, aware of the stillness of the air at midday. It was too hot for birdsong, and the relentless scraping of the cicadas was so familiar that it passed for silence. It crossed his mind that the Medjay might have read it, but then he realised that Maiherpri was only a warrant officer and would have been unable to.

The message was terse; it must have been one of several similar, for it had been copied out clumsily and hurriedly. Huy wondered which of his colleagues had also been recipients. There was a final paragraph which had clearly been inserted just for him.

It wasn't entirely unexpected. The burden of it informed him under the seal of the new pharaoh that scribes and court officials of his rank were being relieved of their duties immediately. Access to their offices would henceforward be denied them, and they should surrender to the Medjay bearing this message any papers, official seals, even jottings on limestone flakes, that they had at their homes. Once relieved of duty they were ordered not to associate with former colleagues again, either for business purposes or socially, on pain of immediate exile. Huy knew that this meant being sent to one of the oases deep in the western desert, the Red Land, or to the gold mines which lay between the River and the Eastern Sea. His personal addition read simply: *See! By the great God, Amun, Father of Karnak, Father and Mother of the Black Land, and by his Embodiment the King Tutankhamun, that you will no more practise your profession, either for the state or in private.*

Huy looked up from this to meet Maiherpri's eyes, where he was surprised to read a guarded sympathy.

'You don't remember me, do you?'

'No. I'm sorry. This is a shock.'

'You didn't remember me before.'

'Your face is familiar.'

'It was before I joined the police. Still in the reign of Neferkheprure Amenophis IV.' Huy noticed that this official was careful to use the name Akhenaten had been born with, not the one he had bestowed upon himself. 'My brother and I were accused of taking barley from the southwestern granary in the Southern Capital. You helped us.'

Huy did remember, and he was surprised that he hadn't before. It had been one of those small, almost incidental achievements—a detour from the normal route of his profession—of which he had been proud. It was seven years ago, for Aahmes had been pregnant with little Heby then. Two teenagers seen fleetingly at dusk, robbing the granary. These two brothers pulled in and accused—such a routine case that Huy, then a rank junior, had been given the paperwork; it hadn't even warranted papyrus, just limestone flakes. But the evidence had seemed to be so circumstantial that he had to object, ask his superior for leave to reexamine it. It had been a lean year, a low flood and a poor harvest. The two young men stood to have their noses and the fingers of their right hands cut off as punishment.

'It wasn't difficult to demolish that case. The granary overseers just wanted a scapegoat. They had been negligent,' Huy said. The Medjay was how old now? At least he understood the lack of deference. It had been familiarity, friendliness clumsily resumed, and Huy had been too guarded to notice it.

'I am sorry to bring you bad news now.'

'Much of it is expected. After what has happened—' Huy hesitated. He wanted to go on, to ask why the new pharaoh had changed his name from Tutankhaten to Tutankhamun, and to ask about the invocation to Amun in the letter. But how far could he trust Maiherpri? The man was a Medjay now, and Huy was an out-of-work junior official of a regime which, with the death of Smenkhkare, was about to be officially disgraced. He altered his tack.

'Have you time for a beer?' Huy remembered his hospitality.

The Medjay glanced at the sun, moving slowly across the patch of blue above them. He relaxed, sat down again. 'Yes. But I cannot stay long, or say much.'

Huy fetched a jar of red beer and two glazed beakers, together with a flat savoury loaf. While he busied himself, he ran over the best way to ask the questions which elbowed their way to the front of his mind, while simultaneously he tried to come to terms with what had happened to him. The dominant thought was that he no longer had a family to share his fall from grace. At the same time, he had never felt lonelier.

Maiherpri took his beer and drank sparingly. 'Of course

there will be edicts. I cannot tell what form they will take. I do know that many scribes of your rank have been offered their careers back if they will deny the Aten and reembrace Amun. The new king expects all his officers to follow his lead.'

'I wasn't offered that option. Not in this letter.' Huy was thinking, the king is nine years old; who is doing this?

'Not all were. I cannot tell why. Many more senior officials have been exiled, and some have been killed.'

'When did all this start?'

'I don't know. They wanted to remove any supporters of the old regime quickly. The renewed God King will be proclaimed in two days, on the day preceding the entombment of Ankhkeprure Smenkhkare, so that he can perform the Ceremony of Opening the Mouth.'

Smenkhkare was sent to join the ancestors in the new Royal Tomb complex at the City of the Horizon. His vault and mortuary temple had been brought into some hasty semblance of completion, though the gangs working there had not had time to clear all their rubble from either side of the entrance, and the Tura limestone of its facings still bore the marks of claw chisels—there had been no time to polish them. There wasn't much of a crowd to line the route from the Temple of the Sun where the cortege set off. Huy saw with regret that already the great building, with its clean lines open to the sky, had been pillaged. It had been the only one to be fully completed within Akhenaten's lifetime, and was his joy and pride, dazzling with colour, as ducks, young bulls, lotus blossoms all in faience-work had danced and leapt vividly and vigorously in the sunlight which they worshipped and which brought them life. Now, most of the men who had worked this miracle of art had dispersed. How fast a thing decays when its life-force is gone, thought Huy. They had embalmed Akhenaten's body, but his ideas, his heart, had been scattered to the wind.

There was little of the simple ritual Akhenaten had introduced in Smenkhkare's burial, which was a reversion to the ways under the old gods. The funeral sledge bore the mummy in its brightly painted cedar shell under a shrine. It was pulled by two toiling oxen along the road to the tomb-rocks, while behind it eight house-servants pulled a second sledge carrying the viscera, guarded by the Sons of Horus: Duamutef, the jackal, for the stomach; Qebhsenuef, the hawk, for the intestines; Hapy, the baboon, for the lungs; and Imsety, the man, for the liver. Alongside the mummy walked two women, court actresses, representing the goddesses Isis and Nephthys, the divine protectresses. Behind the second sledge came fifty women, professional mourners, whose formal ululation filled the dawn sky. Then followed the Nine Friends, and the palace servants carrying the furniture of the tomb, for the use of Smenkhkare's *Ka* who would live there and never leave it.

Far to the front Huy noticed that Meryre, the High Priest of Aten, had been replaced by a man he did not know. Succeeding him were Ay and Horemheb, with the young pharaoh like a prisoner between them.

Huy walked alongside but at a distance, for the crowd was thin except at the entrance to the mortuary temple, and he had no wish to draw attention to himself. At the entrance, the Muu dancers and the Anubis priest in his jackal-head mask waited. The cortege arrived just as the sun broke the rim of the horizon, and the blue-grey light gave way to pale gold. The ululation of the mourners ceased, and as the dancers performed the dance of welcome, Horemheb approached Jackal-Head with the young king. Huy could see that though he was nervous of this, Nebkheprure Tutankhamun was not going to show it. Perhaps he would make a king who could rule even Horemheb, one day.

The attendant priests struggled to bring up the heavy coffin and stood it on its feet, the smooth wood slipping under their sweating palms which left dark marks on it. Then, guided by

Jackal-Head, the new pharaoh reached up and touched the mouth of the old with the Sacred Adze and the Four Sacred Amulets.

'These are the tokens by which I, the Son-Whom-You-Love, open your mouth, your eyes, your ears, your nostrils; put sense into your fingertips and the soles of your feet; lift the gates of the channels of your body: be now as you were in life, watched over by your *Ka*.'

Huy did not stay for the whole ceremony, for the ritual furnishing of the temple, the presentation of the First Meal, and the sealing of the tomb. He felt guilty at leaving so important a funeral, but he was too much a son of the doctrine Akhenaten had taught him to really fear the anger of the old gods for deserting it. He needed some questions answering. Perhaps with official attention deflected to the entombment, he might hope to slip under the rope of the law and talk to one of his former colleagues. He wasn't aware that a Medjay had been especially deputed to watch him, and he didn't think that he was important enough for such attention, but he had to be cautious. Why hadn't he been allowed the option of recanting?

'They think you're a troublemaker, that's why; and of course they're right,' sniffed Tehuty, whom he had tracked down in a dusty archive, luckily far away from anyone else, or the man would never have agreed to talk to him, former brother-in-law or not. 'They want people they can rely on. The old way's dead. It brought the land to its knees.'

'They want people who just toe the line, do what they're told,' said Huy. It certainly made sense.

'Precisely. People *know*. You've overstepped your authority before; you were one of the first to come here when the city was opened. And you're divorced.'

'So is half the population.'

'Not the responsible half.'

Huy turned away in despair. He was never going to get any sense out of Tehuty, whose accusing tone meant that he was going to reduce the conversation to a simply personal one. Tehuty was one year older than Huy, but had been kept back as an archivist for the short and unimportant reign of Tutmosis II while Huy had moved into law reporting. Huy's divorce had sealed his resentment.

'I don't know why you come to me for help. It seems to me you've always despised our family.'

'That isn't true.'

'Why did you leave Aahmes, then?'

'You know why. It had died. She wanted the divorce as much as I did.'

'Well, you've had it now.' Tehuty turned back to the scrolls he was arranging on a shelf and scrabbled at them with nervous, bony hands. Some of them, a hundred and fifty years old, were dry and fragile. 'I'm glad to see there's some advantage to being a simple archivist.'

'But you came here too.'

'I was given the option to recant.' A new thought struck Huy's brother-in-law. 'Not important enough *not* to be kept on, I suppose you might say,' he added with fresh bitterness. 'But I never believed that the theory of one god was anything other than madness.'

Huy tried a different tack. 'What are the changes? What are they going to be?' Tehuty may not have made much of his career, but he was morbidly suspicious as well as jealous, and insatiably curious: those qualities coupled with a highly developed sense of self-preservation and natural subservience made him a perfect spy. If he'd been intelligent, somebody might even have employed him as one.

He could see Tehuty deciding to keep quiet. 'I don't know. If I did, I'd be compromising myself if I told you.' He dropped his voice violently on the last few words, the querulous tone resolving itself into a harsh whisper, for he had heard footsteps approaching from the far end of the archive. But they stopped. Whoever it was had turned off to consult a document on one of the stacks nearer the entrance. 'Why don't you talk to some of your old friends—if you've got any left?'

The last remark went home. In the two days that had elapsed since Maiherpri's visit, Huy had been able to find out very little, except that the three or four scribes, including his former chief, whom he knew he could trust, were no longer at their houses, or under guard and impossible to reach.

'I have heard that certain new edicts are to be made public. Do you at least know when the proclamations are to be made?' Huy tried to choose his words carefully. 'I do need help.'

'You'd never seek me out for any other reason,' said Tehuty. But put into a position of superiority, he relented slightly. 'Yes, I have heard of the new edicts too.'

'And? Will they be read at the coronation?' This was normal, though as far as Huy knew, no date had been set for Tutankhamun's enthronement.

Tehuty looked tense. Someone else had entered the archive, joined the first man at the stacks near the door, and started a conversation. If Tehuty could hear them...He lowered his voice again, to what he hoped wouldn't sound like a conspiratorial whisper. 'There isn't going to be a coronation. There's going to be an investiture. At the same time a regency will be declared, until the king is old enough to reign by himself.'

'Who'll be doing that?

'Can't you guess? Horemheb, though I daresay on paper it'll be a co-regency with Ay.'

'Don't underestimate Ay.'

'It'll be a long time before he can wash himself clean of his son-in-law.'

'But when he does—'

'You love to make deductions, don't you? Have you deduced what you're going to do with yourself now?' Tehuty was reminding him that they were not friends. He didn't want to get drawn into a discussion about the future with Huy.

Huy sighed. 'Is there anything else you can tell me?'

'No,' said Tehuty.

'Does that mean "yes, but you're not prepared to say"?'

Tehuty selected a large scroll and drew it off the shelf, fussily tilting it so that sand ran out of one end. A fat beetle, disturbed, scuttled into the darkness at the back of the stack. Tehuty glanced at Huy and tucked the scroll carefully under one arm before setting off along the dim corridor towards another stack, further away from the door. Huy followed. As soon as he felt he had covered a safe distance, Tehuty turned round and brought his face close. Huy could smell the sweet onions he must have lunched on.

'Well, it's hardly classified, but if I were caught telling someone like you before it was made public, I'd lose my nose and lips.'

Huy resisted telling Tehuty that no one in real power would even glance at small fry like them. He assumed a suitably awed expression.

'They are bringing back the glorious old gods,' he said, a party-liner even in secret. 'Amun will be restored to his rightful place in the pantheon. That is why the king has decided to change his name from the heretical one he had the misfortune to be born with. The trumped-up god, the so-called Aten, will have his name blotted out.'

In the darkness Huy held his breath. The news did not surprise him; Horemheb was a practical man, and it was inevitable that he would select this way of bailing out the sinking boat of the state. The New Thinking had made far more enemies than friends, and the loss of the Northern Empire had accelerated Akhenaten's fall. Nevertheless, and despite the last madness of the old king, Huy grieved. The land belonged to the pharaoh. The people belonged to the pharaoh. The pharaoh could not be questioned. On that order the stability of two thousand years had been based. Now, it had been shaken. Not badly enough to matter for most people; for most people it could be restored, and Horemheb was the man to restore it. But not for Huy. He had discovered what it was to be an individual and to question; and so it was also for himself that he grieved.

He turned to go, but Tehuty held him back. 'There's more. The name of the old king is to be blotted out. His name is to be excised from every monument, in the same way as he excised the name of Amun. Without his name, he will die the death beyond death. He will no longer even *be*.'

Huy faced him with a passion he hadn't thought himself capable of amidst so much stress. 'His name will live for ever.'

'That is capital-offence blasphemy, my friend.' Tehuty smiled his thin smile, and Huy could see that he was enjoying himself now. 'I wouldn't go around saying that sort of thing to just anyone.'

At home ten days later, Huy drew out a copy he had made years earlier, when he had first come to the city, of a description by its principal architect, Bek. He had kept it back from the Medjay. Now he read the short passage once more. It had been an apprentice-piece, and the hieroglyphs were beautifully worked. Its hope and its aspiration seemed to mock him in the dusty courtyard of his little house:

After twelve years, the central part is now complete. Still we have used only one-tenth of the land chosen by Aten for the city, but we rest. Soon, once the enemy to the north has been calmed by the wisdom of Aten, we will begin again. God has only to preserve the king. All our thoughts are on that. Here in the city, we hear little of the world outside any more.

Meanwhile, the city will grow, and it will last for ever. When it is complete, it will be the greatest city on earth. The Southern Capital will crumble to nothing with its false gods and its inhumanity, and the light of Aten will shine on the whole earth. Even the darkness of the north will be dispelled by the light.

How I am looking forward to starting work again! How much

I have to do, now that I know what to do! The city occupies me completely. It must grow like a forest, naturally, with beauty and without symmetry. The columns will be carved with vines and their capitals will be clusters of grapes. Already the palace is covered with paintings—all the animals and all the flowers of the Black Land rejoicing in the one God. The river birds break from the papyrus clumps and escape the fowler. Calves dance in the meadows and deer sprint in the woods. The ceilings and the colonnades are overrun with daisies and thistle, lotus and bulrushes. Each courtyard has a well, and the sakkieh wheels draw water from the River, so that out of the desert here we have brought greenness.

In the hall of a thousand pillars the inlay work is of black granite and red quartzite; the cells of the concubines are decorated with scenes of preparation for the arrival of the king. The painted pavements themselves have been a triumph and a delight to the eye. We laid a mud-brick floor and covered it with a veneer of mortar. We faced it with light plaster bound with the fine hair of girls, and on that we painted. We laid on the colours while the plaster was wet, even when it could still be moved by the brush—form should be as natural as possible. When the painting was done and, dried in, then came the polishers and the waterproofers. The colours will never fade, not when the empire is twice as old as it is today.

We have four glass factories and two glazing works now, but still from the coast the barges bring pottery vessels from Kheftyu and glassware from Byblos. There will never be enough to decorate the palace and the high temple alone. Jasper and alabaster are all the king will have used for his own figurines, and those of the queen and the princesses. But not only that. The votive scarabs, fish and scorpions must be made of nothing less. All richness is here and our craftsmen work with a creativity as fecund as wheat in good silt. The cedar doors are covered with beaten gold.

Throughout the years of building, the king has paced through the city as one pursued by time itself, changing this, altering that, as God moves within him and hones his vision. Grant us only...

Huy let the paper fall. What fools people were to give in to enthusiasms. Outside, the noises in the street were of people packing their possessions on to carts. On the day following the investiture of the young king, General Horemheb and Regent Ay had announced that the court would return to the Southern Capital. The Southern Capital was also the centre of worship for Amun. Work there had already begun on refurbishing the gigantic old palace of Amenophis III. It would be ready in time for New Year, for the Festival of Opet after the beginning of the next Inundation of the River in midsummer. With extraordinary speed, the City of the Horizon had begun to haemorrhage. People flowed from it in search of work, taking what was useful with them. Tehuty and his colleagues were worked off their feet clearing and packing the archives. The buildings of which Bek had written with such pride only a child's lifetime before were already littered with the rubble of their despoliation. Before the autumn was out the place would be a ghost town.

And I will be one of the ghosts, Huy thought. He had no skill beyond the one he had learned, and without that means to channel his natural wisdom, his intelligence would atrophy. There seemed to be very few in his position: forgiveness upon recantation had been the general rule for those who had been in the old king's service—that, or exile or death. Perhaps some such fate would have been his, but for an anonymous superior who must have interceded for him.

The thought encouraged him. His movements were not restricted; he had been allowed to keep his house. But how to earn a living? His stock of beer and wheat dwindled, and he found himself forced to eat barley bread, a minor humiliation at the baker's which nevertheless rankled.

The one thing which had always attracted him as an alternative to a scribe's life was work on the River. Of course to actually contemplate such a move was impossible, as impossible as the thought of moving home without reference to one's superiors, to the system, and ultimately to the pharaoh's needs; but life had unsettlingly changed all that, and now Huy was even—with a certain pleasure which he dared not admit to his conscious mind—willing to throw away the entrenched sense of status his job brought with it. *Be a scribe that your limbs may be sleek, and your hand may become easily wearied, that you may not be extinguished like a lamp, like him whose limbs are soft, for you have no men's bones in you. You are tall and fine-limbed. If you should take up a load to carry it, you would sink down, your feet trailing exceedingly, for you are miserably weak, all your limbs are wretched, and your body puny. Set your mind to become a scribe, an excellent trade, well fit for you. When you call one, one thousand answer. You will walk unhindered on the road, and not become an ox to be handed over. You will be at the head of others.* There had been something like that in one of the early textbooks, but Huy had never liked the implication that it was good to have an effete body—as a by-product and badge of learning. He was unfashionably short and stocky, and his body was naturally well muscled. As for calling one and having one thousand answer, and walking unhindered on the road, that had never been his experience, least of all now. He had ceased to be a member of the exclusive club his teachers had always dangled as the ultimate encouragement.

He took to wandering down to the port, the one part of the city which was still busy, though few boats unloaded here now. The palm piers on their cedar pylons bore a constant procession of copper-coloured men co-opted from the farms on the fringes of the desert, dressed in dirty white linen wraps and carrying endless baskets of possessions aboard the high-prowed barges for the journey south, or revictualling other ships bound to or from the coast, taking cargoes of gold and ivory and granite northwards, and cargoes of cedar, sycamore and Tura limestone south. He would squat on the quay, and as the sailors and longshoremen grew used to him, he would chat to them, or play a game of senet, enjoying their company as a completely new experience, and learning the gossip of the River without the trappings of court politics. But the one time he broached the subject of working alongside them he was countered with laughter so firmly incredulous that he knew he could not insist. He had forgotten for a moment that he had become an outsider who could contemplate breaking taboos built up over one hundred generations.

As his food supplies dwindled he became leaner. In the first month of Shemu, he was down to his last bag of meal and his last jar of beer. The little house was so cheerless that he avoided returning to it except to sleep. Few people remained in his street now, and none he knew. His alternatives were to continue his life as a hanger-on at the docks, or to seek work. The second course was the only viable one, and two or three times now he had packed his few possessions and his scribe's palette before lassitude at the thought of moving overcame him.

He wandered down to the harbour once again. It was evening. He couldn't set off until the morning, he told himself. Wherever it was he was going.

A vast sea-barge was drawn up, dwarfing the jetty, pointing upriver, lightly laden. A gold ship on its return journey. He could see a tall man at its prow, wrapped in a woollen cloak; but the figure was no more than a silhouette against the sun descending in a pool of blood beyond the far shore.

He was turning towards his familiar companions when the figure on the boat called to him by name.

Huy was roused by the cries of the boatmen casting off. He threw off the light rug that covered him and looked towards the high prow which was turning slowly into the River, a group of men there busy coiling the ropes flung off the jetty. In front of him in the centre of the boat, just below the raised rear deck where the cabin was, another team, straining on ropes, hauled the square sail aloft to catch the unfailing north wind. Huy rubbed the sleep from his face and stretched. He was unused to sleeping on hard decks with only the thinnest linen bedroll to lie on.

Now the barge was free, swinging ponderously into mid-stream, its progress controlled by two men working the great rudder oar aft. The sail flapped hesitantly, and then, as the bows cut into the current, filled with wind with the assurance of an expanding muscle. There was a gentle groaning of wood, accompanied suddenly by the sound of urgently. lapping water, and they were underway.

Huy lowered the leather flap of the cabin entrance and sat upright in the gloom. Across the narrow strip of floor, he could see that Amotju's sleeping-place had already been cleared. In the thin pre-dawn light that edged through the narrow air-slits in the cabin walls, he could see the tidied bedroll, and Amotju's sailing kit slung from a hook above it in a linen bag.

Leaning back, he touched his own leather satchel, hanging from a similar hook, in which he had finally stowed the belongings he had neglected to pack for so long. In the event, it had taken him fifteen minutes, no longer, and no more than twice that time to close his house and bid it farewell. And that was how long ago now? He opened the flap again. The gloom was already lifting, and the faintest lilac glow was just discernible in the east. Though the cliffs of the desert were still black, he could see tiny pinpoints of light buried amidst them, as people lit their morning fires along the strip of inhabitable green land on either side of the River which went to make up the long serpent of his country. Dawn might be an hour away, and it had been dusk when Amotju had first hailed him.

Scanning the deck, he could see no sign of his old friend. The cook had struck a flint for the ship's fire, and his assistant was filling a large copper cauldron with water and crushed barley to hang from the tripod for the porage. The glow of the fire as it flared illuminated the cook's greasy, morning face for a moment. Around him the activity of the sailors gradually decreased, as the boat settled into its pattern. Everything had been conducted in the muted fashion in which people work before dawn, and the occasional shouted order or urgent cry of warning had seemed somehow shocking. Huy's other boat journeys, few and far between, and none since he had first arrived at the City of the Horizon, had been on official visits, on state barges. He had never been on a working boat and the excitement he felt overrode the cautious objections another part of his heart had started to issue as he reflected upon the rashness with which he had accepted Amotju's invitation.

Despite the length of time that had elapsed since he'd last heard it, Huy had recognised his friend's voice the minute he'd heard it, and it seemed to him that Amotju had been sent by a god, or at least a protector, maybe by his *Ka*, to rescue him at the precise moment of his lowest ebb. Even so, he hadn't been able to believe it.

'Yes?'

'Don't you remember me?' The voice was light with enthusiasm, and there may even have been a hint of relief. The tall figure in the woollen cloak practically danced down from the prow—Amotju had always been elegant—and was by him on the quay in an instant. 'It must be six years.'

'Since I came here, yes.'

Amotju had never left the Southern Capital. The fleet of six barges he had inherited from his father was based there, plying the River south and north with mixed cargoes, but always going south to pick up gold, and carrying it on downstream as far as the Delta, where it would be transferred to the sea-going ships which carried on the coastal trade. The barge from whose deck he had hailed Huy was the flagship. On the rare occasions when Amotju travelled with the fleet himself, it was on board *Splendour-of-Aten*.

'Now back to her old name,' smiled Amotju. '*Splendour-of-Amun*. One has to move with the times.'

'What are you doing here?'

Amotju smiled again, more fleetingly. 'An important cargo. A big shipment to the Northern Capital. And my best captain suddenly sick. The important thing is that if I hadn't come, I'd never have met you again. What are you doing?'

Wondering how far he could trust this friend after such a long gap, Huy filled in as many details of his life as he felt prudent; but there was no avoiding—and as far as he could tell, no need to avoid—telling him about his lack of work. Amotju's keen dark eyes had already been scanning his undeniably shabby appearance, and no doubt that told its own story.

'So, what is there left for you to do here?' asked Amotju when he had finished.

Huy shrugged. 'Very little.'

'With no job and no family, I would have thought that this was a very good place to leave.'

'But I cannot leave without a reason.'

'Might you go north?'

Huy read his thought. 'There isn't any question of returning to Aahmes.'

'You do have a reason for leaving, though. This city is finished. In a year, it will be empty. In another, the desert will reclaim it. It will be a place for the rats and the dead.'

'That is true. And yet, I cannot tell you what hopes we built up here.'

'They are gone. You must look elsewhere.'

Huy couldn't deny the truth of all this. Perhaps he had just needed someone to tell him. Those members of the court who had not already departed to long-neglected residences in the Southern Capital, where Horemheb was already busy supervising the rebuilding of the palace, had accompanied Ay and the pharaoh downriver on a state visit to the newly appointed Vizir of the North. The only stop they would make here on their way back south in the summer would be to collect the city supervisor whose job was to seal the tombs of the great in an attempt to protect them from robbers until it became possible to ship their bodies to new homes being prepared for them in the Great Valley of the Setting Sun on the western bank of the River, opposite the Southern Capital.

'You look as if you need a wash, a shave, food, wine, a woman—maybe two women—and work,' said Amotju. 'The first four we can provide here. The last we can discuss. The other is up to you.'

Putting an arm around him, to the astonishment of the longshoremen, who saw their former gaming partner and dock layabout taken up by one of the most powerful lords of the River, Amotju took him aboard. As soon as he set foot on the planking. Huy knew that he wanted to leave, to go south on this boat, and to seek whatever crumbs fortune might throw him. For the first time, as he looked back from the ship to the dark, lifeless outline of the city in the dusk, he felt that his future was no longer here. He was clinging to nothing, unless he himself turned grave robber, and even then, he thought drily, the pickings were richer to the south.

'The supervisor here has a soft job, sealing the tombs from robbers,' he said over the first glass of Kharga wine—Amotju had always spent his money discerningly, so he was not surprised to be drinking the best. 'As far as I've heard, all the grave thieves have been working in the south, in the Valley, since Akhenaten moved the court up here.'

Amotju looked troubled. 'Perhaps you should come and see for yourself,' was all he said.

'I might. One day.'

'Let it be soon.' Huy noticed an eagerness in his voice which he couldn't possibly ascribe to friendship; after all, Amotju had more or less ignored his existence for six years. He told himself to be more charitable. They had both been building careers, in cities two days' river journey apart.

'It cannot just be chance that we have met again,' Amotju said later. 'Why don't you seize the opportunity, and come with me now?'

'I am not one for quick decisions,' replied Huy; but he felt his pulse quicken. Two pottery wine jars lay empty at their sides as they sat cross-legged opposite each other on the stern-deck, their faces lit by the last fire of Ra as he slipped behind the Hills of the Dead.

'There is nothing to keep you here; everything to draw you there.'

Huy felt his blood race, finally. In all his life everything had been fixed, certain, but the last few months had been like wandering in the desert, and he was tired of it. Here was a chance. He would take it.

'Why not?' he had said.

He had refused Amotju's offer to send men to collect his gear—no strangers could have found his house through the maze of dark streets. Amotju had been astonished that Huy was prepared to go alone, however; and Huy was reminded that even he had not entirely shaken off the fear of the ghosts that lurk beyond the firelight, or of the disembodied dead, those unfortunates without memorial statues, whose mummies have been rotted with water, and, having no dwelling-place any more, must seek another, by tearing out the heart of a living man and eating it. Akhenaten had dismissed such beliefs as stories concocted by the priests; but the traditions stretched back to beyond the time of the pyramids, and they were a thousand years old. Huy had agreed to an escort, though the rational part of his heart told him that Amotju was sending the men with him as much as anything to ensure that he did not change his mind.

Leaving home fast had been salutary, and left no time for sentiment or regret; having the boatmen there with him had helped, too; but he would not have changed his decision. His little house was cold and dark, unloving and unloved: it too had become a ghost. The time of his life in it was already long past. He took his expensive ox-leather satchel and into it put the two or three remaining papyrus rolls he knew he could not do without, and his scribe's palette, some ingots of gold that had survived, and, after hesitation, the small statue of the house god, Bes, the little protector whom Aahmes had made him promise always to keep with him, with tears in her eyes, at their last meeting.

After he had closed the door on the courtyard he turned his back on it. He had not taken a last look round. He had not said goodbye to the places where he had formerly been happy. That happiness was a ghost, too. His mind turned to the warmth of the company on board, to the dinner of roast duck and millet. The moon was up already, Khons in his chariot, turning the sand that had already drifted against the walls of the deserted buildings a soft silver. He breathed in the velvet air, clutching the Eye of Horus at his neck, which had always hung there despite the influence of the New Thinking, and hastened his step towards the tiny lights outlining the barge.

Amotju was one of those people upon whom life had consistently smiled. So great had been his fortune that from time to time these days he could not suppress the worry that he was tempting providence and that the day when his luck ran out was increasingly likely to be sooner rather than later. Inheriting from his father not only his fleet but also a level-headed sense of business and a strong instinct for self-preservation, he had managed never to commit himself to either side during the troubled years which now seemed to be coming to a close. The service his business provided was too essential to any politician for him to come to harm by hedging. All he had needed was to be unfailingly polite, and to give an impression of being charming but dim—and therefore not to be feared. Now that the heresy of Aten seemed to be thoroughly scotched, and the old gods back in their place, he began to feel that he could drop some of the pose and reenter the political arena. But his instincts told him to keep his mask in place.

He'd done so admirably, but, as he told himself ruefully, even the most cautious man can't help twisting his ankle in the occasional pothole. In his case, the pothole was a girl called Mutnefert. A girl? A woman! A tall, slender woman, whose father had come here from Mitanni—she had the high cheekbones of that race.

He summoned her into his mind and undressed her there, appraising the dark copper of her skin, her long legs, high buttocks, hips narrow like a boy's, though her breasts were firm and full. She had broad shoulders, her back was muscular, and her arms had strength in them, unlike the soft arms of the court ladies he had known. Unlike them, too, she wore her own hair, not a wig, washing and lightly oiling it so that it shone. Her hair was not black like a pure Egyptian's, but a deep chestnut, and straight and soft. Her eyes were large and dark, though the whites of them were dazzling; and they seemed always to be keeping something to themselves. Amotju caressed every detail in his imagination, and as he did so he knew that he could not give her up, could not abandon the fight to possess her completely; but with that thought a shadow crossed his heart. As if anyone could possess her! It was she who would choose; and at the moment she did not choose to abandon her principal lover, the priest Rekhmire, guardian of the shrine of Osiris at the Southern Capital, and overseer of the reconstruction of the palace.

Powerful as he was, Amotju did not have either the contacts or the resources of his older rival, who had become tougher during the years in which the old priesthood had been driven underground, out to the oases and far, far to the south, or into the desert as far as the coast of the Eastern Sea. Returned to power, even within half a year, the followers of Amun had breathed new life into the Southern Capital. They had a pharaoh and a general who supported them again—Horemheb had started publicly to worship at the shrine of Osiris as soon as he had returned from the City of the Horizon. Amotju thanked his *Ka* that he was not a victim of the witch-hunts pursued against the followers of Aten.

How far Rekhmire himself suspected that he had a rival, Amotju did not know. Mutnefert would permit no discussion of the other part of her life; but he knew her to be discreet, if only for her own sake, and from the passion of her lovemaking he could not believe that she was not a woman worth taking risks for. Nevertheless, a month earlier he had been taking the food offerings to his father's tomb late in the day, with only one servant to accompany him. It was a duty-visit, for Amotju was rich enough to hire mortuary priests full-time to perform this function; but he owed his father much, and could never be sure that the *Ba* of old Ramose did not hover over him reprovingly at times. Amotju therefore chose to propitiate the old man's *Ka,* more powerful than the *Ba*, but at least unable to leave the tomb.

That evening there was no one in that part of the Valley, though two tombs nearby had been recently sealed and should still have had guards posted. Yet there had been someone else there after all, for they had heard whispering, seen the glow of torchlight reflected on a rock, and the tiny avalanche of rock and dust that had cascaded down nearby was too great to have been made by an animal, even a light-footed jackal. Having only one servant with him, Amotju had decided not to investigate. Once home, however, he sent a man off to report the incident to the Medjays, and gave orders that for the time new guards be placed on his father's tomb.

The next morning, though, he awoke to find something to make his heart jump in fear within him. Hanging in a little woven cage, from the very window-frame of his room, was an ichneumon, the little eater-of-crocodile's-eggs which he had venerated as his personal god since childhood. The diminutive mongoose twisted and turned in distress within the confines of its narrow cell, and was further disturbed as its movements made the cage swing in the air, and it missed its footing on the wicker floor.

The animal was unharmed, but round its neck and around the front right paw strips of red linen were loosely tied. The significance was clear. Amotju, forcing himself to breathe deeply and regularly to keep fear at bay and quieten his pumping heart, cut the cage down and, after cautiously removing the swathes of linen—worship did not safeguard you from being bitten—took the animal to the River to release it himself, taking care that no one saw him, before telling his household that he would be leaving that day, taking personal command of *Splendour-of-Amun*. Very few people knew about his personal god, and how they could reach him through it; and if they were powerful enough to deliver a warning to the very heart of his house, they were people to respect. Amotju's instincts told him to disappear for a while; but this was to be a strategic retreat. Whoever's enmity he had attracted would have to be flushed out and fought. Amotju never once thought of giving ground. He had decided on the river journey to give himself time to think, to decide which of his friends he could enlist for aid. It hadn't been pure chance that he had docked at the City of the Horizon. He had not forgotten Huy; even as a child, when they had shared the same tutor,

Huy's father and old Ramose being friends too and having married sisters, the little scribe-to-be had been a problem-solver. From what he had heard, that penchant hadn't ceased with the years. Amotju's informants had told him that quite unconsciously, but not at all surprisingly, Huy had frequently invoked the fury of his superiors by questioning poor or unjust decisions. It was only by some very discreet and judicious string-pulling that he had been able to save his friend from the sentence of exile that had been recommended for Huy immediately after the death of the pharaoh, Smenkhkare.

'Who do you think is after you?' Having heard as much of the story as Amotju chose to tell him, Huy, who had been watching the western bank of the River scud by as he listened, with its little knots of white villages and palms punctuating the green strip, turned to his friend. It was midday, and they sat under an awning amidships. Apart from the helmsmen, the rest of the crew found shelter from the sun in what shade they could. The wind had slackened, the sail wallowed resentfully, and the barge made slow progress against the stream.

'Hardly the grave robbers. I don't think they were even aware of our presence.'

'But there must be a connection. Did you see anyone else between returning from the Valley and going to bed?'

'No.' Huy noted the fractional hesitation in his friend's voice. 'I'm trading on long acquaintance; but did you go to bed alone?'

'Yes.'

'Isn't that unusual?'

'No. My wife and I no longer do anything together; she runs the household, controls the business accounts, and is happy. And I don't need to take a concubine every night. If I had, I would have sent her back to her quarters before sleeping.'

'Let me think for a moment.' Huy turned back to his view of the riverbank, moving slowly, so as not to offend his friend. His thoughts for the moment were for himself.

He was being offered an opportunity to work, and his heart was as grateful for employment as a thirsty gazelle in the desert is for an oasis pool; but this employment was strange. He could see that this was no matter for the Medjays, whose lower ranks could keep order on the streets and investigate attacks on traders and even boats, but whose upper echelons had always been the instruments of the pharaoh and the state; and he was unable to resist the lure of a problem to solve, as Amotju had thought and hoped, but he hesitated; where would the work lead? His eyes were screwed tight against the sun and he used this to glance across unnoticed at his friend busy mixing water and wine. Amotju was his age, but the gods had shaped him tall and sleek, given him money and position, safety and power. He sat there, cross-legged in his pristine kilt, again of wool, not linen, pouring the good Kharga wine. Few lines marred his face, the kohl round his eyes was immaculately applied. He owned this very boat, and five more like it, on which Huy would have been grateful to have just a job. His marriage, though apparently dead inside, was still at least intact, and he had his children. He also had five concubines, twenty house-servants, and who knew how many slaves and paid skilled men in his fleet. He seemed like a man whom nothing could shake; and yet...

Yesterday, as they had sat on board together in the firelight and dined, the duck meat heavy on Huy's stomach as he had not eaten such food for months, Amotju had painted a rosy but vague picture of Huy's future. He had waited to broach the real reason for taking his friend with him so precipitately until today, when the boat was well on its way; when there was no turning back.

And yet Huy would have had to move, had to have done something. Clearly Amotju needed his help, or thought he did, badly enough to ensure that he couldn't do anything but give it.

Perhaps his friend was just an instrument of fate after all. He watched the eternal sunlight dance on the water, catching for a moment the metallic turquoise of a dragonfly as it darted-and-paused across the surface.

Huy rubbed his belly. At least he would eat well for a time if he took this job; and he knew already that Amotju had said enough to hook him, and that Amotju had more to say, if he could only coax it out of him. He turned back.

'What have you heard about the new king?'

Amotju was taken aback. 'He is our lord.'

'He is very young.'

'What do you mean?'

'He is a child. It will be four years before he rules. Then, those in a position to find themselves in favour with him will be fortunate.'

'I say again, what do you mean?'

'That the time to build is now.'

'But what has that to do with the threat of my life?'

'To build, people need funds. Tell me more about Rekhmire.'

Amotju poured wine. On board, he liked to do these things himself. 'Are you reading my heart?'

'I would just like you to tell me what you have not told me.'

'I have told you all that I know.' Amotju had deliberated about whether to do more than sketch in the details of his relationship with Mutnefert. He had not said that she was also the mistress of Rekhmire, though he had hinted at a rivalry between the priest and himself.

'No, you have not.'

'I—'

'If I am to help you...' Huy paused.

'It is true that for a man who half a year ago had little but his former reputation, Rekhmire has built up wealth with astonishing speed. Of course, he has been careful; he has graded the increase of his affluence so that it will seem natural, but even so,' Amotju concluded.

'And what does he buy?'

'He buys people presents.' Amotju could not keep the resentment out of his voice.

'Meaning, he buys people?'

'There are those who have the ear of Horemheb.'

'And of the king?'

'The king! He is not there yet; he is in the Northern Capital. Besides, he is a child, he will do what Horemheb tells him —' Resentment had brought the words out in a rush; this was not at all what Amotju had planned. Nevertheless, his need to trust somebody was stampeding him into taking Huy into his confidence far more quickly than he had intended. He poured himself more wine. The heat of the afternoon, as the *Seqtet* Boat of the Sun began its downward journey to the west, beat through the linen awning. He pulled off his wig, and ran a hand over his head before wrapping it loosely in a shawl.

'But does he need to? He is already a man with power,' Huy persisted.

'That power he has already bought.'

'Nevertheless, he cannot have built up so much so quickly.'

Amotju was committed now; he decided to ignore the notes of caution sounding in the back of his heart, and to bring Huy completely into his confidence. Huy would not use the knowledge to buy back favour for himself; their friendship was too old for that.

'Come on,' said Huy, half humorously. 'I know you and secrets. You have never been able to keep one for long.'

'I cannot keep them from those I have decided to trust,' replied Amotju, 'but you must swear by Horus to keep what I will tell you to yourself.'

'I cannot swear by the old gods; but I cannot do the work you ask of me unless you tell me all you know, even all you suspect.'

'Then I think that the death threat came from Rekhmire. If there were any way of proving that, he would never have sent it; but success has made him very confident and he has little time left before the pharaoh arrives in the Southern Capital. The people expect it and even Horemheb cannot thwart them for ever.'

'Why has he so little time?'

Amotju made a gesture of impatience. 'You have been away for a long while. You must be prepared for many changes now that you are returning. For a decade the city has been in decline. After the court left, there was no rule. Only the old priests who stayed on gathered what remained of the reins of power, and used it to their own ends. The Valley was left unpoliced. The tombs of the great pharaohs lay there, unprotected, full of riches; gold mines on their doorstep.'

'You mean that Rekhmire—'

'I can prove nothing. Of course there were gangs formed of the men who used to quarry out the tombs; they knew the layouts, the false passages. But one group has been operating to the exclusion of the others. They take little, but they take the best. They store it somewhere in the Valley and they must get it away by river. But their time is running out. Horemheb is back, and he is galvanising the army and the Medjays. He wants to restore dignity to the ancestors and through that to give pride in itself back to the Black Land. Grave robbers who are caught now are impaled on the west bank of the River and left there to be picked clean. Rekhmire will have to close his operation soon; but he will sail as close to the wind as he can.'

'Using the grave goods to buy influence with Horemheb!' Huy smiled. 'This may be a deadlier snake than Apopis. I think what you ask of me is more than I can do.'

'You will have all the support you need. But of course you will not live at my house, and you will work alone.'

Huy did not say that that was how he would prefer it. He also realised that if the investigation misfired, Amotju would not know him, and the death that would be given him would make him look on impaling as merciful.

'Give my work a name,' he said, finally.

'Bring down Rekhmire.' Amotju did not add his private

reason for wishing this. It was enough for Huy to think Rekhmire a political rival and no more; in the same way he had not given voice to his suspicion that the death threat stemmed less from his having disturbed grave robbers than from the priest's jealousy of Mutnefert. Amotju hadn't told Huy that he'd visited his mistress on the night he'd returned from visiting his father's tomb.

Huy was working to subjugate his own pride. 'And give my work a price,' he said.

'If you succeed, you may name it.' Amotju smiled, and poured more wine. Already, he felt, as the alcohol worked on him, they were halfway towards his goal.

Huy's feelings were very different. He was thinking of this time tomorrow, when *Splendour-of-Amun* would be docking at the Southern Capital. It seemed as if the cold hand of Set closed over his heart.

It was as if he had never been away. Still far downstream, the low cliffs of the great buildings could be sensed rather than seen as they rose from and blended with the land that surrounded them. As the barge drew nearer, Huy could see that the garish paintwork had faded, that statues had fallen, and pylons cracked. He wondered what the town to the south of the temple complex would be like. He remembered the teeming narrow streets behind the broad boulevards, the confusion of the markets, the sour fishy smell of the docks. He noticed that several ferries toiled between the east and west banks, between the city of the living and the city of the dead, across the broad grey-brown sweep of the River.

So familiar, and yet so alien. He had lived the first twenty-three years of his life here, and now he was returning to it a stranger. There would be few who would remember him, or acknowledge him if they did. But that might be to his advantage, given the work he had to do now.

As the barge made its approach and the boatswain stood in the prow ready to blow his horn to warn the traffic of their arrival, Amotju beckoned a sailor over.

'When we dock,' Amotju told Huy, 'I will disembark first. There will be people from my house to meet me and if I am seen arriving with a stranger there will be questions. You will wait on board until the unloading is under way, and then leave with Amenworse.' He indicated the sailor, a heavy-shouldered man who looked like a northerner. 'He will take you to a safe lodging.'

'You are well organised. Did the gods forewarn you that you were going to meet me?'

Amotju grinned. 'No, but in my business I have occasionally carried special passengers who did not wish attention to be drawn to their arrival or departure; so there are always contingency plans. But don't worry. I will send word on ahead to let them know you are coming.'

'Can I ask where that is?'

'Let it be a surprise. You will be in good hands. I will join you there later.'

After he had gone, Huy sat on the rear deck, watching the work of unloading: sacks of barley, rough-hewn cubes of white Tura limestone for Horemheb's rebuilding programme, cedar logs from the lost empire bordering the Great Green Sea. Despite the thinness of the cargo, it was late afternoon before the work had finished. Huy had aimed to use this time to plan, to set out a strategy of campaign in his heart, but now as the sun sank once more he found that he had done nothing, thought nothing. Instead there was a well of panic in his stomach that not even the wine which Amotju had left him could fill. Indeed, he did not feel confident enough to drink. It was clear that for all his protestations, Amotju did not yet trust him; and for his part he could not trust his former school-fellow either. The sailor, Amenworse, joining in the work of unloading with the rest, kept throwing him sidelong looks, and Huy wondered how much he had been told. To look busy he had taken out his palette and doodled on a limestone flake like a clerk checking and noting the offloaded stores.

Finally the work was done. Before the sailors not deputed to remain on watch left the boat, bound, if Huy knew them at all, directly for the brothel district, Amenworse beckoned him. They were to leave together, concealed in the stream of people descending the gangplank.

Waiting for them close by was a light rickshaw with its collapsible superstructure of linen—to protect its occupants from the sun—still up. It was not the only one on the rectangular patch of beaten earth a few steps up from the quay. Amenworse and Huy would attract no more attention than anyone else catching a ride into town.

As soon as they were aboard, the two rickshawmen ducked under the towing bar, hoisted themselves in down to waist-level, and as the car behind them tilted, eased the vehicle forward and broke into a brisk trot. Huy noted that there had been no discussion of fares or a destination named.

As soon as they left the quayside they were enveloped in the clutter of streets, hedged in with mud-brick houses, the more prosperous of which had wooden doors and lintels. Many of the houses were severely run down, their walls scarred where the mud-stucco had fallen off, and the dreary brown colour of unrefreshed whitewash; though as many again were draped with flimsy palmwood scaffolding. The road was of hard-packed earth, for the town was built above the level of the River at its highest point of inundation, and Nut rarely shed tears for her happy people—so paving was unnecessary. At this time of day, few were about; people would either be at home or back at work after the afternoon rest. In the open squares which punctuated their route, traders had laid out their wares on sheets: pitchers of palm-oil, cosmetics, dried fish, dates; and in the shade butchers protected their meat from the flies and the sun by wrapping it in wet linen. Through gaps in the houses and at the end of lateral streets which made straight as a die for the shore, the passengers could catch glimpses of the sandstone cliffs of the great buildings, the ones built by the God Kings to last for ever. The façades teemed with workmen as the city prepared its renaissance.

Huy looked at the straining backs of the rickshawmen, their heads wrapped in loose sacking turbans, as they hauled their way up the broader road which sloped gently out of the city centre towards the larger, less cramped houses of the merchants. Here he had often come as a boy to play as Amotju's guest in old Ramose's villa, and here little had changed. There was none of the sense of decay he had half expected, though it was true that several of the mansions stood empty, their gardens and fishponds neglected. Along the streets, palms and the occasional fig tree provided sparse shade, and great tanks set into the ground, laboriously replenished by slaves carrying jars filled at the River, ensured enough water to keep the whole area constantly green and cool.

They turned off finally and for several paces ran the length of a high, blank white wall, coming to a halt by a door painted ochre, adorned with the protective *ankh* amulet. Here Amenworse, who hadn't spoken a single word to Huy during the whole time that he had been in his charge, jerked his head at him to indicate that he must alight.

'Where are we?'

A repeated jerk of the head.

'Whose house is this?' Then Huy saw that Amenworse was not looking him in the eye, but at his lips. The sailor's eyes then rose to meet his, and in turn he opened his mouth, and nothing came out but a strangled chaos of sound. Without speaking further, Huy slung his satchel on his shoulder and climbed down to the path. He could feel the late afternoon heat through his palm-leaf sandals.

No sooner had he descended than the rickshawmen padded off and he was left alone in the silent, sunny street.

He was about to knock on the door when it opened, swinging inwards on silent hinges, to reveal a pleasant formal garden, with lotuses surrounding a rectangular pool in which large dark fish brooded. Standing back from the entrance was a servant-girl wearing a long shift, copper bracelets and ankle-rings. Perhaps this was Amotju's place after all, and he'd been brought to the back door.

Then he saw her.

The last time they'd met, she would have been twelve. What a difference six years made, though at the time she had already been beautiful, and old Ramose had been entertaining three prospective husbands. He wasn't in a hurry to marry her off though, because she would bring a good dowry with her, and he hadn't wanted to see it go far from the family. If he had had his way he would have married her as a secondary wife to Amotju, who was after all only her half-brother; but her mother, though only Ramose's chief concubine, had set her face against it. Ramose had grumbled terribly at the time, but since the death of Amotju's mother, his chief concubine had become his favourite, and he found himself unable to deny her anything. There were no cousins, and so Ramose had still been undecided on the matter of a husband for his daughter Aset, since she herself, in the stubborn manner of her mother, had refused all the suitors presented to her, at the time of his death.

Huy had seen her before she saw him, as she stood in the doorway with her head partly turned towards the interior, talking to some person invisible within. He could see instantly from the style of her hair and the way her dress was folded that she was not yet married; and he was half surprised to find himself excited by knowing this. At the same time he was uncomfortably conscious of being hot and dusty from the journey, and wished that he could have bathed and changed before meeting her. As she turned to descend the short broad flight of steps to the garden, he saw the closed expression on her face, the slight frown which, he remembered, appeared when she was confronted by an unwelcome task; and he wondered how often Amotju had imposed his secret passengers on her in this way. He wondered, too, what her reaction would be when she recognised him. If she recognised him.

But she did so immediately, her brow clearing like the sky after night and her dark eyes widening in disbelieving pleasure. Four servants, three girls and a man, had followed her out of the house, and they took their cue from her smile, visibly relaxing too.

'Huy! What wind blows you here? My brother said to expect a guest; he did not say it was to be a pleasure.'

'You flatter an old man.'

'Come in; and do not pretend to be more of a fool than you are!'

She took his arm and led him into the house. He felt the light pressure of her hand and wondered if in truth it was possible to be more of a fool than he was; but years had washed by without a woman and the smell of her caught and teased and stung in his nostrils. A dream, of course; but no less pleasant for that. As she showed him his room, and as the servants undressed him and poured jars of cool water over him in the bath, fatigue and doubt and worry slipped away.

'Amotju says you can tell me everything. I am honoured, of course. But tell me what you have been doing since I was a little girl.'

'That is a very long story, and there isn't time for it.'

'But I hope you will stay long enough to tell me.'

Aset's skin was pale but her eyes and hair were ebony; she was small and light-boned, and there was still much of the child in her movements. She seemed to have so much energy that she danced rather than walked. A keen intelligence shone from her eyes and it illuminated her oval face, which was framed by hundreds of slender plaits. Her hands were strong, like her brother's, and there was a determined set to her chin. Huy was reminded of Aahmes, before her face had become so constantly sad.

'What do you do with your time, Aset?'

She smiled mischievously. 'I run the vineyard my father left me. Amotju cannot understand it. He thinks I will never marry.'

As he talked to her, he found the plan which had been eluding him all afternoon beginning to form in his heart, though not without effort. But the questions she asked were the questions he needed to stimulate him.

'Will you want to meet Rekhmire?'

'Yes. Can it be arranged?'

'It is possible. But he is a very important man now. He has already abandoned the work on his tomb on the edge of the Valley, and they have started a new one for him, grander, nearer the centre where the kings lie. When would you like to see him? What pretext shall we give?'

'Not so fast,' said Huy. 'First I need to feel the pulse of the city. I have become a stranger here; I can't just go blundering out into the streets. If there is a case for Rekhmire to answer, it must be constructed. So far all I have got is one story from your brother.'

'Where Rekhmire is concerned, my brother jumps at shadows.'

'Do you know anyone else who might have threatened him?'

Aset was silent.

'Are you thinking, or do you have no answer?'

'I am thinking that, after all, no harm has come to anyone.'

'Amotju took it seriously enough to leave. He did not bring me back here to amuse himself.'

'He is becoming a politician, now that he sees order settling once more on the land. And he jumps at shadows.'

'So you have said. But are they shadows?'

'That is for you to find out.' She looked at him.

Somebody had seen him arrive; somebody must have done, and perhaps even recognised him, for, as he walked in the street in the centre of town, a tall man in the crowd blundered into him. He was gone again before Huy could react but he had left a souvenir—a tiny slip of papyrus pressed into a fold of Huy's cloak. On it was written simply the name of a tomb in the Valley, together with the word, *tonight*.

Huy knew the name. This is quick work, he said to himself. He had not been back in the Southern Capital for more than three days. The question was whether the message was a warning from a friend or the bait for a trap from a foe.

There was nothing else on the papyrus, not the slightest clue. Huy knew that all he could do was go up to the tomb and watch. What else he might do if anything happened, he didn't think about for the moment. His military training was long behind him, and he did not possess so much as a dagger. Perhaps, after all, nothing would occur. But it was unlikely that this scrap of information would lead nowhere.

He decided to tell no one. There had been nothing to report yet to Amotju, but his friend was not impatient, and was now involved in arranging an audience with Rekhmire for Huy, a job which, in the convoluted politics of the Southern Capital, involved the use of contacts at the third remove. Huy had also asked Amotju to arrange a house in the city and a body-servant as soon as possible. He would take them as advance payment for his services. He had not told Aset of this. She would be offended, and press him to stay; and he would be tempted. But the truth was that he was used to his own company, and thought he needed solitude.

He would not tell Aset about the papyrus either. This was the toughest decision he had to make, for the man whose tomb was named was old Ramose. Huy told himself that whatever happened there, it was already guarded. Perhaps the note simply alluded to a rendezvous, the sender mentioning a tomb whose location Huy would certainly know.

He would cross on the ferry at dusk, though he burned with impatience to get over there now. In the afternoon, the Valley, despite the palms that had been planted there in profusion, was the sun's anvil. Apart from the tomb workers, busy in the cool caves they were quarrying out from the rock, no one would be there.

Evening saw him on the west bank, the buildings there already throwing long shadows towards the River. Keeping to them as far as possible, for he had no official business here and needed to avoid being challenged, he started the long walk to Ramose's tomb, which he remembered from the time when it had been under construction, and Ramose himself had taken him with Amotju to see it. The builders had tunnelled out an imposing entrance hall, which was to be dominated by a statue of Ramose, beyond which an ante-chamber led to the chapel, with its blind door for the *Ka* to come and go from the tomb itself, which would be at the bottom of a vertical shaft cut six paces down into the rock. At the time, the halls were bare of the rich painting with which they would now be decorated; but there was no doubt that this was the tomb of a very wealthy man; and Ramose's pride had been so evident to the young Huy that he had envied him for his own father's sake.

He walked on, past the last workmen's huts, now deserted, and up towards the silent city, carved into the rocks, where the great dead lived. He had no fear of them; they existed alongside the living, happy if they were respected and fed the ritual meals, if their names were remembered and spoken. But the silence up here awed him, and the black pools of shadow in the rock seemed capable of harbouring all the demons in *The Book of the Dead*. Walking as softly as he could, the noise of his feet on the stony desert floor nevertheless seemed deafening, the clack and tumble of the stones certain to give him away.

Night fell swiftly, and would have been absolute, had it not been for a slender moon which Huy was grateful for. Although it made the shadows even more fearful, and intensified the silence, he could not have found his way in the utter darkness of a moonless night. Now he could look back down upon the city, its outline etched on the desert, by the moon. A few fires flickered, their light at this distance almost too feeble to reach him.

He wondered about the guards Amotju had set. The men who undertook this work were often ex-soldiers, or said they were. They commanded high prices and yet it was hard to check that they did their work.

Huy could not envy anyone who had to spend their nights here for a living. A bat swooped down, quick and silent, close to his head; taken by surprise he ducked, tingling with fear. Then, after waiting a moment to steady his breath, he went on. It could not be far now, for he had reached the outer edge of the tombs—where the very rich were allowed to rub shoulders with the least of the royal family. Only the most influential and favoured of the priests and politicians could break through this enchanted circle.

Reaching the next crest of rock he saw the tomb entrance below him. As he had hoped, he had come upon it at an angle where he could see before he was seen. Now, he pressed himself into the shadow of the rock wall—a friendly shadow, he told himself wrily—and peered into the little arena formed by the wall of rock into which the tomb had been cut, and the low parapet of dressed stone which curved out on either side of it to form an almost circular courtyard.

The moonlight was concentrated here, and Huy could read the inscriptions around the door: the name of the dead man, the invocation to Ra, the invocation to Horus and to Osiris; the prayer for food and the prayer Not-To-Be-Forgotten. The door itself was expensive, of massive cedar inlaid with bronze. Unless it was well guarded, it would be cut up and carried off itself, Huy thought; let alone that which it guarded.

Spoiling the effect of this was a crude shack, hastily thrown up against the rock to the right of the door, and from which a dim light glowed. So there were guards.

The normal method of operation for grave robbers was to tunnel through the soft rock from the outside, directly towards the mortuary chapel where the chief treasures were laid up for the dead to enjoy through his *Ka*. Entrances were usually concealed—old Ramose could never resist show—but even here the corridor beyond would probably be booby-trapped. Unless you had knowledge of the locking mechanisms, even if you got beyond the door in the pitch darkness of the entrance hall, you could find yourself thrown down a shaft, or crushed or cut off from your goal by a sliding stone portcullis.

Huy settled down to wait for he knew not what. He had walked far and his feet ached. If he strained his ears, he could hear, but not distinguish, the muffled conversation of the guards. But in the first hour, no one emerged from the shack. He glanced up at the moon, measuring the progress of Khons' silver chariot over the dark roads.

He must have slept, for when he looked again, the silver chariot was high and thin, and he was cold to the centre of his stomach; but something had awakened him, some sound. Associated in his heart with a dream it had shaken him out of, he could not name it. Then, as he struggled to remember, it came again. The sharp dry bark of a jackal, curiously loud, and nearby, somewhere below him to his left. Almost immediately, there was movement within the shack, and two men emerged. Huy wondered if anyone could be left inside but decided that the size of the shack made it impossible, unless it were a dwarf.

At the same time, figures detached themselves from the shadows at the entrance to the courtyard. There were three of them, huddled, shrouded almost, so that it was impossible for Huy to tell much about them or see their faces. They had moved silently and fast, but now hovered at the edge of the shadows. Despite himself, Huy felt his guts knot in fear. Below, the first of the guards was clearly suffering the same emotion, going into a half crouch, scrabbling for the short sword at his side. The other, who held a pike, seemed to hesitate, and looked not at the creatures in the half-dark, but at his friend.

With a sudden surge of energy that leapt from his bowels to his mouth and tore his stomach away, Huy saw what was going to happen, even as the second guard continued to hesitate, even as the central one of the three figures detached itself from the shadows.

The words came out as a terrible falsetto shriek, a voice that was bubbling and frothing over with madness, and a lean arm rose and pointed. Huy instinctively raised his own arm, cried out a warning, but his limbs were made of lead, his mouth full of linen. The figures below played out their roles before him like actors in the slow dance of a pantomime as the second guard seemed taken over by a power beyond him and made a small, deliberate lunge forward, transfixing the first on the pike, which, like the good soldier he must once have been, he then twisted and tore upwards and outwards. Blood followed the blade in an impatient black gush.

The first guard stood looking at it, a frozen statue, no part of him moving except the blood pumping out of him. Already the figures were moving forwards, past him, towards the door, ignoring him. The second guard had flung down the pike and was joining the others at the door, where one of the figures was confidently searching the carving on the left for the stone bolt which, once withdrawn, would leave the tomb at their mercy. And if they were so certain about where that was...

There was nothing Huy could do to stop them, but if he ran, he could try to get help from the tomb workers' settlement below. If they believed him; if they could be bothered to turn out. For a moment he considered waiting and letting the robbers enter the tomb, then closing and sealing the doors behind them. But they were already pushing one open, and it was taking three of them to do it. It was time to make his move.

The hand that crushed his shoulder was made of bronze.

He was lifted off his feet and hurled against the rock behind him, then pulled out of the shadows again. He smelt foul, asphyxiating breath, an odour of long-dead fish and sulphur. He gasped and closed his eyes; something enormous, hard and yet animate, like a vast muscle, was pressing him into the rock, suffocating him. He could no longer feel his arms or legs; his whole body was one mass, one centre of pain. He made himself open his eyes, and found himself staring into a face that appeared to be made up of green stones; a long-jawed face with gimlet eyes, and a great red mouth in which a sinuous tongue voluptuously rolled. A face he remembered from the scrolls of *The Book of the Dead*—the face of the demon, Set.

The High Priest of Osiris, Lord of the Underworld, sat at a low table in the large room prepared for him in the palace. The palace was the mightiest ever built: Amenophis III had reigned for thirty years in wealthy peace.

Rekhmire's mother had been in charge of the south linen store here, and he could remember playing in the grounds as a ten year old, three decades earlier. There was no question of restoring the whole building. The façade facing the River was seven hundred paces long, and behind it the clusters of big, rambling buildings stretched five hundred paces inland. There was no end to the harem suites, servants' quarters, offices, kitchens, workshops and storerooms. It was a city in itself, and there was no possible way in which the new young pharaoh and his diminished retinue could fully occupy it. There was no revenue to restore it all either, even if there had been the need.

But this was not what was preoccupying Rekhmire as he sat poring over the rolls of papyrus spread out on the table in front of him, a bewildering mass of information covering everything from absenteeism among the army of unskilled workers and craftsmen to the cost of the dyes used in the repainting of the walls of the royal quarters, and the replacement of Amenophis' name with Tutankhamun's.

Try as he might to concentrate on his work, Rekhmire could not rid his thoughts of Mutnefert. She possessed him! What had started as a civilised affair like any other had become a passion, and he knew that the passion was one-sided. Yet, the cooler her treatment of him, the more he burned. He reflected on what he risked losing if he placed himself too much in her power. She was unscrupulous, he knew; and he was not certain that she was faithful to him. There was no question that she could do him harm; but she might make him look ridiculous, occasion him loss of face; and that was something his career and his pride could not stand. He had already taken enormous risks to come as far as he had, and so fast, since the reestablishment of order under General Horemheb, whose ear he had; but Horemheb did not need him. He was not indispensable, and there were far too many willing and able to step into his shoes.

He had considered having Mutnefert killed, just to be rid of her; for to exile her might have placed her outside his physical reach, but not outside the bounds of his imagination. He could not bear the thought of her with another man, though frequently, despite himself, he would torture himself with the contemplation of it. And yet, to kill her...He still could not bring himself to have it done. He had wondered about having her watched; but he knew that if she discovered such a thing she would be done with him. At the same time he did not think he could bear to have confirmed what he most feared.

He turned once more to the papers before him, picking up first one and then another, and placing them in loose order, at least to distract his mind; but desire had taken hold of it, and he knew that he would not be able to work until he had satisfied it. Cursing inwardly, he pushed his seat away and pulled himself to his feet, picking up his wig and jamming it roughly down on to his broad skull as he limped to the door to call one of his body-servants. The bad foot was more swollen than ever in the heat, and it ached sullenly as it dragged after him.

The slave came running. He had a hard young body which shone in the sun, and Rekhmire laid an appreciative hand on his muscular shoulder. Perhaps this boy would do...But no! He needed a woman, now, to slake his lust. Then he could work. Tonight, in his own house, in the room painted with the act of creation, he would make Mutnefert earn her keep, earn her place as his mistress. Somehow he would find a way to break her proud spirit, and then the thought of her would cease to torment him. As his heart dwelt on what he would do, he caressed himself gently, his breath ragged.

'Master, shall I—?' asked the young slave.

'No. Get me a woman. One of the foremen's whores will do, as long as she's young. But get her quickly!'

There was a roaring noise, like much water driven through a narrow channel, only muffled and distant. He wanted silence, but the noise would not diminish, and there seemed to be a slapping, a beating, too, as of paddles, except that the two sounds were one.

He longed for the silence that there had been before, but the racket would not let him return to it. To shut it out, he contracted his eye muscles. A hundred paces ahead of him winches twisted and solid doors closed. Ochre suns burst in front of his eyes, and amidst them a man dangled on the end of a pike. Many leagues below his eyes, his lips began to move. A rank taste, but coolness. The words: eyes, lips, seemed like new discoveries too. Then there was breathing. But breathing hurt. It was too much effort. If only the noise would let him drift back.

It was no good. He had regained consciousness, and the pain had to be faced. If only it would be granted to him to get over it before there was fresh danger. He made a cautious movement—new discoveries: arms, legs, a pelvis—though all too far away to contemplate. Remote; not his, not really. But as he moved, a hundred thousand freezing needles drove outwards through his forehead, through the top of his skull, and a lolling sac of bile lurched in his stomach. The top of his skull; he wanted to tear it off, to let air in, then there would be relief.

He knew that he had half raised himself on to one arm, but now he was stuck. He wanted to lie back, but couldn't face the pain of more movement. His whole body would burst; everything would run out. His head hammered and great yelps of pain whanged round it with each beat of the distant mill race. It was as if embalmers had already broken through the ethmoid bone and driven their thin hooks up his nostrils into the cranial cavity to remove the brain. He tried his nose, to breathe there, but it was caked solid. For a moment panic banished pain, but then he discovered his mouth again, and breathed there, not gulping, taking it slowly.

After a moment or two of this his heart began very falteringly to grow steady. His body reassembled around it and he stood once more at his own centre. I will stay here, he thought, until something happens. If nothing happens, I will stay here for ever. This will do. This is at any rate better than it was. Meanwhile his heart and memory trawled for scraps of the howling dreams that had occupied—how long? It seemed several lifetimes since he had climbed up to Ramose's tomb.

After another minute had passed he realised that although his arms and back retained the impression of stone and rock, he was lying on something softer, and something soft was covering him. He did not yet know which direction was which, or whether he was upside down, but at least he was no longer floating in a void where the teeth of the creatures of the pit tore at him.

There was something else. Something that was not of him, but outside him.

A touch.

It resolved itself as a cool hand on his arm. Lying there gently, with just enough pressure to reassure, to say: I am here.

'Aahmes...' He wondered if he had the strength to open his eyes. Very slowly, he relaxed them., The exploding suns were gone. Through the coral membrane of the lids, he could see real light.

Someone was calling him. Gently, cautiously. Calling his name. But he still could not open his eyes. He had to decide where he was, whom he might be with. Very gently, the hand moved on his arm, stroking it, reassuring. Another touched his brow, and from the movement of the body he could now clearly feel close to him there came the delicious scent of seshen.

He blinked. The light in the room was dim, yet it shrieked into his pupils, scalding the retina. The freezing needles returned, stabbing frenziedly. He reached out and held the hand that had been on his arm, holding it hard, for dear life, to keep control, and it held his in no less firm a grip.

When the room had ceased to rock, and the yelling in his skull had subsided to a dull but manageable throb; when the bed seemed unlikely to lurch and pitch him on to the floor, he opened his eyes again, firmly this time.

He looked into another pair of eyes, concerned, raven-black.

'Osiris has sent you back to us,' said Aset. Huy could not remember the last time that a voice had held such tenderness for him.

Much later in the day, when Amotju had joined them, he told them of the circumstances which had led him to the tomb. In turn, he learnt that he had been unconscious for three days. They had found the body of the murdered guard first, lying where it had fallen in the courtyard. It was not until they had examined the pillaged tomb that one of the household servants found Huy.

'We were worried that you had disappeared,' Amotju explained later, when Huy was able to sit up and take food. The three of them sat on the garden terrace of Aset's house that evening. Huy felt luxuriously wrapped in its safety, and enjoyed the deep pleasure that only comes with the sense of having survived great illness or great pain. 'But we had no idea who might have known about you, or wanted to get to you so quickly.'

Huy told him about the papyrus note.

'Someone recognised me, or had seen me leave your boat. So, either some enemy of yours suspected me of being a newly-hired agent and wanted to waste no time in getting rid of me, or some friend of yours knew about the grave robbers' plan and wanted to warn you through me.'

'The first seems unlikely; and in the second case, why not warn me directly? There is another thing.'

'Yes?'

'Why did you go alone? Why did you not tell me?'

'You do not want to be associated with me publicly, remember? I am a disgraced officer of Akhenaten.'

Amotju was silent.

'And the tomb? Your father's tomb. How much damage was done?'

'Little damage. They took everything that was expensive. Everything that was of wood and everything that was of metal. Some *shabti* figures. They tried to prise the bronze from the doors, too. I am having the doors covered by a stone shutter. But damage—no. These people do not desecrate; they simply take. Did you see their faces?'

'No.'

'How did they know you were there?'

'They must have had lookouts whom I did not see.' Huy was not prepared to describe his encounter with the demon. He could not accept that such a creature could even exist outside the imaginations of the priests; that it would abet tomb plunderers seemed even less likely. So he kept silent. This was something he had to resolve in his own heart before he spoke of it to others.

'Do you hurt still?'

'I hurt.'

Aset had sent for a doctor as soon as Huy had been brought back to her house. The doctor had located three broken ribs, a torn muscle in the shoulder, and said that there had been much loss of blood. 'Three hours longer, in the sun, and he would have died, dried up like an apricot.'

'The world must know I am here now,' said Huy. 'Perhaps it is time for me to move.'

'It doesn't matter now if the world knows you are here, or that I know you. It is too late.' Huy could sense irritation in Amotju's voice. 'You should not have gone alone. You should have come back here and relayed a message to me through Aset. Now, you may have startled the big game away by frightening the hares.'

'If they knew who I was. There may be no connection between the people who gave me the message and the people who robbed the tomb. I was just someone in the way, a stray worker, a tomb-servant, another guard. They left me for dead; it is their misfortune that I survived.' Huy smiled. 'Have you yet been able to arrange a meeting with Rekhmire?'

Amotju frowned. 'It is never easy; but yes, he will see you. He is looking for a clerk of the works for the southwestern quarter of the palace; but do not worry,' he continued, catching Huy's expression, 'he will not engage you. He will sense your independent spirit and he will not like it. Don't worry, my friend; I know what your fate would be if you were caught acting as a scribe again after the work had been forbidden you. I would not expose you to such a risk.'

Huy relaxed. 'There is another question, which becomes urgent. I can no longer stay here. If I proceed deeper in this, there may be risks to Aset.'

'There are no risks I cannot face,' said Aset.

'I have considered this request of yours,' said Amotju. 'And for the moment I prefer that you stay here. In any case there is no question of your moving now. You have had a battering, my friend. I want you to recover quickly, to finish the job I brought you here to do. Aset will see to it that you are better cared for than any manservant would, and alone you would neglect yourself. You have been foolhardy, but perhaps your presence at the tomb scared them, prevented them for doing even more harm; and for that I—we—are grateful.' He rose, draining his cup of wine. 'Take care of him, Aset. Huy, can you walk?'

'Yes.'

'Then come with me to the gate.'

As soon as they were away from the garden terrace, Amotju dropped his mask. His expression was troubled. 'First the death threat. Now, the robbery at my father's tomb. Can they be linked? Is Rekhmire behind them both?'

'I will find out.'

'Do. Recover quickly. I feel an ill star rising over me.'

'We create our own ill stars.'

'No. The gods do.'

Amotju pulled his cloak around him and mounted the litter which awaited him at the gate. The four body-servants who attended him picked it up by its four handles, and bore him off into the dusk. Huy stood for a moment at the gate, aware that the door-slave was eyeing him curiously, but unwilling to re-enter the house. He drank in the rich air and watched the darkness engulf the last moments of day. Under the bandages, he could feel the soreness of his body, but he had no intention of resting. He had been caught, humiliated. It was a lesson from which he had been lucky to escape with his life. Now, he was going to find out who had tried to take it. It wasn't just Amotju's political interests he was serving any more; it had become his own fight, too.

He walked back towards the house. The night was warm and kind, and the scent of the flowers hung heavy in the air. From a bush, a bird murmured sleepily.

There was no one on the terrace now but Aset. She had moved to sit on a long couch which had been placed at the edge of the pool. With a stick, she idly teased the slow-moving fish, dark as the water.

She looked up at him as he approached, and there was a new light in her eye.

'Sit here, next to me.'

He did so, aware more keenly than ever of the warmth of

her body. She was wearing a long, loose shift, gathered with a carelessly tied girdle at the waist.

'Do you really want to leave here?'

'It would be better if I was in the city.'

'You can't wait to get away from me.' Almost a little girl's voice—and yet, of course, calculated. She leant forward, swirling the water gently with her stick. As she did so, the material of her dress stretched across every contour of her body. He placed a hand on the couch next to her, his throat dry, but she continued to tease the fish, looking down at the water in complete concentration. After a moment she leant back and smiled at him, looking at him directly, challengingly, with those night-black eyes.

'When I was twelve and you were twenty-three..." she said, still smiling; but it was a very certain kind of smile now. Idly, she relaxed her legs, her right hand toying with one end of the girdle. She brought her naked left foot up and just touched his knee with her toes.

'I don't want you to go away,' she said. 'I've been watching over you for three days and every day I have wanted you more. Do you think you—? When you came back to us this morning, the first word you said was Aahmes.'

It had been three years since Aahmes, and longer than that since he had been close to a woman. Already they were beyond words and beyond caution. He was holding her foot, caressing it with his thumb, and then her calf, her knee, her thigh, pushing the shift up, as she loosened the girdle and let it fall away. She lay back on the couch and he leant against her, feeling the sweet joy of her flesh against his as her hands worked at unfolding the tucks of his kilt. His ribs ached but their complaints came too late to stop the desire. Her arms were round his neck, caressing the back of his head, as he brought his lips down to cover first her right breast, then her left, softly sucking the nipple she thrust into his mouth, teasing it with his tongue, nibbling it with his teeth. She brought his head up to hers and held it for a moment, looking into his face with the eyes of a passionate stranger; then their lips were together, their tongues stroking and wrestling each other, as she pushed and rubbed her body against his.

Her arms were busy around him, and he realised that she was gently manoeuvring him to her side.

'Lie still,' she whispered, her hands on his flanks now, and her mouth kissing, licking, exploring his neck and upper chest, then darting much lower. He felt her fingers form a tight ring around the base of his penis, before she drew it gently into the warm wet cave of her mouth, to meet the caresses of her tongue.

He would have liked to spend longer exploring her body; her hard thighs and tight buttocks; her soft, challenging breasts, the delicious moist cavity of her mouth; and later there would be time, but now, their need for each other was too urgent—as urgent as it was spontaneous. He drew her up to him again and rolled her on to her back on the couch. Her hand was below him now, reaching hastily to guide him as he lifted his body slightly away from her, listening to the contrast between his own ragged breathing and her sighs and gasps. In another moment they were one.

Huy was trying to fathom the priest. He could not have provided a stronger contrast to the ascetic, unworldly men who had guided the worship of the Aten in the City of the Horizon. This man had his feet planted firmly on the earth. He was heavily built, though not tall, and might have been anywhere between forty and fifty years old. One of his fleshy shoulders rode considerably higher than the other, and the face that hung between them on its short neck was coarse, loose-lipped and pock-marked, though the eyelashes, exaggerated by kohl, were long and curiously feminine. The overall impression was of a man in love with power and in love with himself in that order. A politician and a survivor who would not care who else sank, so long as he rose to the surface himself. Huy wondered whether he was vulnerable to anything at all.

They sat opposite each other in Rekhmire's room at the palace. For his part, the priest kept his counsel. He knew that the man sitting opposite him had all the qualities the job he had in hand demanded—he was a good scribe, and had sound knowledge of engineering and architecture. Here, too, was an independent spirit which it might be better to have under his own wing, on his side, as it were, than in the potential employ of any of his enemies. Of course he couldn't be sure that the man wasn't that already, and sent as a spy.

'It will take time before I make a final decision,' he said finally. 'Where can I reach you?'

'I will contact your clerk. I am new in the city, and not yet settled.'

'Then I advise you to find a house quickly. You must register with the Medjays.'

'It is stricter here than it was when I went away.'

'Yes...You have not said why it is that you have returned here from the Delta.'

'My wife and I have divorced.'

'I see.' Rekhmire did not enquire further. He allowed the silence to descend again.

Huy wondered what he would do if he were actually offered the job, but decided that the likelihood of that was remote. He was well aware that the man opposite him didn't like him; that he presented an obscure threat to his sense of security. It had been worth the risk to get close to him, to get his measure; but the task of collecting evidence against him, enough to bring him down, would be as great as laying siege to a city.

Two days after this interview, and five after Aset and Huy had made love in the dusk of her garden, the bullion barge *Glory-of-Ra* was wallowing in midstream halfway between Aswan and Esna, on the sixth day of her journey downriver after taking on a cargo of Nubian gold. This late in the dry season there was little activity on the farms which sporadically lined the banks of either side of the River, and this was in any case a lonely, underpopulated stretch. With a valuable load on board, the captain, Ani, one of Amotju's senior commanders, had taken on a detachment of Nubian marines as private guards, and these were now deployed at the bow and stern, armed with bows and lances. The River was broad and sluggish here, and even with every man at his oar, there was no way the overburdened *Glory-of-Ra* could outrun or outmanoeuvre a lighter, faster craft. So far, the voyage had been mercifully uneventful; but still Ani anxiously scanned the horizon of the River ahead and behind. Even to carry off part of his cargo would make rich men of river pirates, and a man on horseback could have carried news of him ahead from Nubia much faster than he could travel.

The sun had risen two hours above the horizon, and he was beginning to think after all that they had sailed too far upriver to fear attack, when his forward lookout hallooed that there was a sail. Ani squinted ahead. Behind him, neatly stacked in the broad open hold, the gold, mostly cast in rough ingots from moulds dug in the sand, and as yet still impure, shone dully. On either side, along the narrow strip of deck, his crew were taking up their positions by the stowed oars.

For a moment the light was too bright to allow him to distinguish the pale tan of the advancing sail from the sky, but as soon as he had it fixed, he knew that he should prepare for the worst. This was no trading ship coming upriver to meet him, but a light merchantman, of the kind used for speed along the barren coast of the Eastern Sea, and also for war. As the pharaoh's pennant did not fly from the mast, this was not a naval vessel on patrol.

There was no avoiding the encounter, so the next hour was taken up with preparations. A huge linen tarpaulin was hauled over the cargo, and the Nubians stationed themselves about the prow and along the two forward sides of the barge, taking their bows and jamming their quivers upright next to them. The sailors released the oars, more to use as weapons or hindrances to a boarding party than to row with. The stream was with them, and that was an advantage; but on the other hand, the light boat approaching could run rings round them if it wanted to.

In contrast to the long wait, the attack when it came was swift and unannounced. The two boats had not yet drawn level when from the prow of the oncoming vessel an arrow hurtled, striking one of the forward seamen in the neck. A lucky shot. The man keeled over and fell on to the tarpaulin covering the hold as if he had been poleaxed, his blood spreading rapidly over the dirty white linen where he lay. There was no time to react, however, for this first shot was followed by a hail of arrows, clattering as they glanced off the sides of the barge, or thudding into the wooden deck. In that first volley, two more sailors and a marine fell. One had taken the arrow in his stomach, and the marine had been hit full in the mouth. Blood gushed out, and he stared at it in disbelief before his eyes clouded. The other sailor had been shot through the shoulder, and now rolled on the tarpaulin next to his dead fellow, howling in agony until Ani told the boatswain to get down there and pull the arrow through and out.

Glory-of-Ra began to return fire as the distance between the two ships closed. The pirate was striking her sail in order not to overshoot, and Ani realised that she meant to come alongside and grapple to his barge. Hastily he gave orders for the men on that side to put out their oars and stave off the other boat. He could see the enemy now, but their faces blurred. They were rough-looking men, the kind of sailors he'd pass over when selecting a crew. He'd have liked to feed the lot of them to the crocodiles.

With a rending and splitting of wood, two oars snapped as the weight of the pirate ship crashed against them. The sailor holding one of the oars was tossed into the air, where he executed a perfect forward somersault before falling between the two boats, the moment before their sides smashed together. There was a splintering of more oars, and above the cries of the men, a snap like the crack of a whip as a great wooden blade sliced through the air and connected with the nape of the neck of one of the pirates, a large, swarthy Syrian with a prodigiously hooked nose.

The marines had abandoned their bows and were thrusting forward with their lances, skewering with a cold, deliberate movement any of the enemy who came too close. For a moment they pressed forward, and Ani dared to hope that they would succeed in holding off the attack for long enough to enable his sailors to rally. He grasped his own bronze short-sword tighter and hacked at the wrist of a pirate who was gripping the deck-rail. The man jerked back with a howl of pain and shot Ani a look of such venom that the captain momentarily recoiled. It was going to be kill or be killed.

The thought sent a wave of panic through him as he scanned the scene in front of him, trying to assess their chances. There were a great many pirates, and they continued to appear. Some of them must have come from the far north originally, for they wore beards, which, as a good Egyptian, Ani abominated as hot and disgustingly unhygienic. They wore their own hair, too, which was lank and dirty.

'Come on, throw these buggers off!' he roared to his men. The marines were still holding their ground, though they had not made progress and two more lay dead. As for his sailors, their defence was feeble and weakening. Scarcely were the words out of his mouth than Ani realised that they were going to lose. What was more, these pirates had no intention of grabbing what they could and making off with it. They were going to take the whole ship. That meant they would take no prisoners, and make sure there were no survivors.

As he came to this realisation, another marine fell. The clamour around him could now be divided between the aggressive, increasingly triumphant cries of the pirates, and the howls of his own men. The marines fought silently, but when he looked at them, he could see that their expressions were set and grim. Blood ran along the decks and the water around the boats was slimy with it. Bodies floated near the interlocked hulls. Ani scanned the shore for crocodiles. It would only be a matter of time before they put in an appearance, attracted by the smell.

The current had borne them towards the shore, and now the boats were jammed against a sandbank which ran just below the surface of the water. The pirates would have a job getting *Glory-of-Ra* free, and without her they would have to be content with as much of the prize as they could carry in their smaller craft, thought Ani, realising at the same time that he had given up the fight.

He wondered if he could organise a retreat. If he could get at least some of his men to the shore, it might be that the pirates would make off. He couldn't expect help from any of the tiny villages along this part of the River, but they had come too far downstream for there not to be a sizeable town soon, and the pirates, even if they succeeded in getting *Glory-of-Ra* free, would have to take her downriver, not up. Even with a sail, she was too heavily laden to make the journey south.

He looked along the shore again, and saw a group of men on horseback watching the affray from a small sandstone prominence not twenty paces away. There was absolutely no doubt about it. They were Medjays.

'Help us!' he yelled. He was not the only one to have noticed them, for several of the sailors had turned away from the fight and were now facing the immobile horsemen, wailing and waving their arms beseechingly. Only the marines fought on, though they had been forced further and further back, and eight of them lay dead.

The Medjays remained immobile. Meanwhile, taking advantage of the sailors' distracted break in rank, the pirates swarmed over the side of *Glory-of-Ra* with a roar. Those who were not cut down scuttled across the deck and hurled themselves into the River, oblivious of the other threat from the crocodiles which were now launching themselves lazily into the water from the opposite bank. Ani fought on, continuing to call for help and looking in the direction of the Medjays with increasing disbelief. At last he, too, dived into the River. It was dark green and opaque, swirling with activity as the crocodiles feasted on the dead. Praying to Nekhbet to protect him, he swam underwater, hoping to reach the main current and be carried downstream.

'But you can't give up now.'

'Can't I? I have had enough misfortune. It would be foolish not to heed the warnings.' Amotju turned away and looked out through the broad open window that overlooked the town and the River. Behind him in the room Huy spread his hands and said nothing.

'The loss of the gold is much; don't you want to find out who was responsible?'

'The shipments are secret. Only one man is powerful enough to extract that kind of information. Rekhmire. He has proved himself too powerful for me.'

Word of the battle had come down from the villages, and no doubt the story had been exaggerated in the telling. Exaggerated and obscured, for the Medjays whom Ani had seen so clearly were described doubtfully as 'a group of horsemen'. From the crew of *Glory-of-Ra*, it was said, there had been no survivors. Those bodies which could be rescued from the crocodiles had been hooked and hauled onshore. Their families could console themselves that, dying in the River and eaten by Sobek's children, their souls would be doubly blessed. In addition, they could expect payment in consolation from Amotju. The pirates, unable to dislodge the barge from the sandbank, had plundered it as best they could and rowed off downstream. They had vanished at some point before reaching the Southern Capital, and there had been no sign of their vessel.

'Besides, the loss of the gold is not so great that it outweighs my sense of self-preservation.'

'If you let your enemies know that they have got you on the run, they will be unremitting. Now is not the time to retreat.'

Amotju motioned to a servant to pour wine, and as he took it Huy saw that his hand shook. He drank the cup down fast, and had it refilled.

'The gods are against me; I will not tempt them further.'

'And Rekhmire?'

Amotju looked at him. 'I will not hinder you if you wish to pursue him. But that is all.'

'This is your fight, not mine.'

Amotju, Huy realised, was not the confident, strong creature of business and politics he had taken him for. It was possible, too, that these were the first misfortunes life had ever brought him, and they were coming too thick and fast for his liking. It must have seemed like the fulfilment of a prophecy.

'We still only have political rivalry as a motive for Rekhmire's attacks on you. Surely that isn't enough reason? If he is as powerful as you say, why should he not simply...remove you, if he sees you as a threat?'

'Better to ruin me than remove me.'

'He has a long way to go, then.'

'Meanwhile, he fills his treasury at my expense.'

'Then let us stop him; but I will need more than financial support from you.'

Amotju had turned to look out of the window again, and now a puzzled frown crossed his face.

'What is it?'

'One of my seamen. He's running up here as if Set were after him.'

A matter of moments later the man was ushered into the room, bringing the smell of the River and his own sweat with him. Amotju recognised him as a boatswain in one of his smaller barges, which had been engaged in the work of refloating *Glory-of-Ra*. The work had had to be undertaken quickly, for left unguarded the barge was a prey to pilfering by the local villagers. It had been a poor flood that year and the fields had yielded a mean crop. Thus the farmers could not withstand the temptation of such a prize despite the harsh punishments for theft which Horemheb had decreed in the young pharaoh's name.

'What is it?' Amotju asked the man.

'Sir, Ani has been found.'

Huy and Amotju exchanged glances. His was one of the bodies not recovered, and it had been in both their hearts that, however unthinkable, he could have been an accomplice.

'Alive?'

'He is more dead than alive, sir. He got away from the slaughter on the barge, but one of Sobek's children tore a leg off below the knee. Some peasants found him and tended him.'

'Where is he now?'

'We brought him back with us. They are taking him to the Place of Healing. The wound is clean, but needs to be dressed and examined by the doctors.'

'But how is he?'

'The peasants took good care of him. They expect a reward, for they knew who he was. He still had your seal round his neck and they must have recognised it from the ships.'

Amotju glanced at Huy. 'Let us go and see what he can tell us.'

Ani was lucky not to have joined the ancestors, and that there was food enough available for the crocodiles not to have pursued him downstream. If he hadn't brushed against an animal and stimulated the attack he might have escaped entirely; but the River had caught him up the moment after the mighty jaws had crushed down and torn his leg free of his body with a pain so searing that he passed out. That he hadn't drowned was due to a twist in the current which had swept him round a bend and on to a narrow strip of beach before he could take too much water into his lungs; but he had lost much blood before the peasants had found him.

'And you are sure that they were Medjays?' Huy asked him, after he had given them his account of what had happened.

'Yes. At least, they wore the tunic.'

'Did you recognise any of them?'

'I couldn't take in details in the heat of the fighting. But one who sat near the front was tall for an Egyptian, and broad-shouldered. I noticed him because he sat so still in the saddle, just watching us die. He might have been from Mitanni, or Syria. He had high cheekbones. But I can't tell.' Ani's face flickered between Huy's face and Amotju's. He was exhausted, and clearly could tell them nothing more.

'Thank you. You are a brave man,' said Huy.

The three men fell silent.

'What will happen to me now?' said Ani, hesitantly. The tone of his voice indicated how fearful he was of the answer.

'You will rest,' said Amotju. 'When you are well, you will take a command again. You do not need two good legs to manage a ship.'

As they left the Place of Healing, Huy thought that despite his earlier doubts, his friend was still someone worth fighting for.

That night, Amotju lay with his eyes gratefully closed, his face close to her warm breasts, her arms safely around him, protecting and comforting.

'You are good to me,' he said.

'I don't expect you always to come here simply to perform,' replied Mutnefert. 'Sometimes it is better to talk.'

Sighing, he opened his eyes and disengaged himself from her long enough to pour wine and drink it. Mutnefert watched him. She wore a long tight gown, but she had not offered to take it off nor had he asked her to, and she was relieved, for though they had subsided, she did not want him to see the bruises on her back and buttocks. Rekhmire had been more violent than usual. She had thought of an excuse—a fall from a horse that she rode side-saddle, for pleasure; but she did not want to have to use it. It was good that he had come to her tonight simply for comfort, and to talk.

She reflected that for all the attraction of his power, the sacrifices she made for Rekhmire were too great. If only she could trust herself to do without his protection. Sooner or later, she would have to find a way out of that labyrinth; but not now, not tonight. Now, she would think of other things. She stroked Amotju's head, and bent over and kissed it, gently, enjoying her own kind of power. It brought its own problems, but she was glad that Amotju had come to her with his tonight, and unburdened himself of them. She loved him.

The snout of the monster pushed itself out of the molten copper and nudged his leg; but he knew he was safe; he was hovering just above the liquid in the blackness. If he chose, he could fly higher, out of reach of the snapping jaws. For a moment the snout withdrew slightly, dipping below the surface which closed over it like mercury, leaving not a ripple. He hovered where he was, watching the smooth copper mirror just below him, courting danger, excited and repelled by it at the same time. Why didn't he have the sense to fly higher? Some madness prevented him.

At that instant the snout appeared again, lunging out and up, without hesitation this time, the jaws opening as they broke the surface. He was looking straight down into a red mouth edged with seven rows of ragged teeth, like the flint blades of embalmers' knives. The lolling tongue, like the giant larva of some other prodigious beast, lay ready to embrace him, dissolve him, to eat away at the tissue of his body with its saliva.

He had to get away now, to fly straight up, beyond the reach of those vile jaws. He could see the eyes now—the whole head was revealed. Human eyes staring from a face made of rubble; eyes with thick, woman's lashes. He flapped his vulture's wings and they beat upwards—against a ceiling. He had not known, had not seen it or sensed it above him in the blackness, but he was already against it, pinned there. The jaws snapped at air a hair's-breadth below his naked belly. He could feel the rush of the wind they made as they closed, and smell the choking odour of long-dead fish and sulphur which blocked and caked his nostrils so that he could not breathe. He could see the beast swimming below him in the murk, gathering its strength for a second attack, the eyes looking straight up at him with a flat stare. No pity, no mercy, not even enjoyment— just calculation. Vainly he flapped his wings, but he was tiring, and the monster knew it. When it dived, he knew it would be in order to shoot up vertically from the copper-water again, and this time he would fall headfirst into the vile maw. Already he could feel the coldwarm, sticky fondling of that tongue.

His shoulders ached with the effort, of keeping himself aloft; for a moment he closed his eyes to concentrate his strength. When he opened them, the creature had gone. It had dived. But even before he had time to react, it came roaring up through the water and engulfed him.

Huy awoke trembling, and for eternal seconds the dream remained with him, the cold wet surrounding him belonging to the narrow cave of the creature's throat. Then he moved, cautiously, and felt the bandages tight around his chest were sodden with sweat. He felt his bedlinen also soaked through. He tasted the velvet night with his lips, and found comfort there. Opening his eyes, he saw the distant gods of the night riding far away in the sky, at giddying heights above the clouds in their shimmering chariots of electrum and gold.

He sat up, removing his neckrest from beside him carefully so as not to awaken Aset, who lay curled up next to him, turned towards him, one hand under her face, sleeping as a child sleeps, her own neckrest abandoned in favour of a bundled-together sheet. He climbed down from the sleeping—platform and walked to the window. The relief at having escaped from the dream overwhelmed him. He had told no one of his encounter with Set; could not believe that it had been anything more than a charade—and yet, why? Who was he to say that there were not gods and demons who walked among men? If Akhenaten had been right, and the only god was that expressed in the sun's light, why had people rejected him? Was he wrong, or was it simply that people preferred the dark ways to the light? Perhaps people themselves were creatures of darkness.

He looked back towards the bed. Sensing herself alone, Aset had turned in her sleep and lay on her back, the sheet thrown off, one leg stretched out and the other bent and spread to the side. She looked terribly vulnerable. Huy considered, reluctantly now, that he would have to discuss the matter of leaving again. He had exercised extreme care in his comings and goings, and in all his meetings with Amotju. Apart from members of Amotju's and Aset's households, no one knew where he was. He had contacted Rekhmire's office, to be told (to his relief) that he was not required for the post. Indeed, they had looked up his background and he had been issued with a sharp warning not to solicit work which had been forbidden to him. This was another relief. Had he been so minded, Rekhmire could have had his nose slit for such presumptuousness.

But if he wanted to delve further, he would have to be free to do so; and he could not take the risk of Aset or her house being put in danger.

He did not yet feel he could trust sleep again; it was not impossible for gods to come to men in dreams. He crossed the room to a table set against the far wall, and poured himself a beaker of red beer from a jug set next to a bowl of yellow figs. It was too dark to read, he did not want to disturb Aset by lighting a lamp, and he did not want to be alone in another room either. He took the beer back to the window and sipped it, looking out at the River, black and silver beyond the huddle of the town. The silence was absolute, and not even a watchman's fire glowed on the distant quays.

Aset stirred again, and shivered. He went to spread the sheets back over her. As he did so, she awoke. The trust in her eyes as she looked at him was almost more than he could bear.

'Are you awake?' she asked him, sleepily.

'Yes.'

'Can't you sleep?'

'I had a dream.'

'It must have been a nightmare.'

'I have forgotten it already.'

'Then you must sleep again.'

'Not yet.'

'There is nothing you can do tonight.'

He sat on the bed. 'I am trying to think around what Ani said. He said there were Medjays watching the attack.'

'Then they will never be found. The police may look for the pirates, but not for their own people. If there were Medjays, it wouldn't be the first time that the police had turned a blind eye to a crime in order to get a cut.'

'Who do you think was behind the attack?'

She raised herself on one elbow, took his beaker of beer and drank from it. 'No one. River pirates exist.'

'This had the makings of a naval attack.'

'They have grown bold,' she replied fiercely. 'There has been no order on the River for years. General Horemheb has not taken power before time.'

Huy preferred to ignore her last remark. It struck a discordant note which he didn't want to admit into their relationship. 'Nothing to do with Rekhmire?'

'Amotju swears that Rekhmire is behind it, of course.'

'And you disagree.'

She looked impatient. 'It is possible; but Amotju is obsessed by that man. Of course they are rivals; but I do not think that my brother would take it so seriously if it were simply a rivalry for power. That he well understands. At present he is in the grip of something he does not understand, and cannot control.'

'And what is that?'

Aset was surprised. 'Why, love.'

It was Huy's turn to be taken aback. 'What do you mean?'

'Hasn't he told you?'

'What?'

'If he hasn't told you, maybe I shouldn't say.'

Huy took her by the shoulders. 'Don't keep me in the dark. Tell me.'

'I think it would be better if he told you himself.'

'Then I must know what question to ask.'

She looked at him. 'Ask him about Mutnefert.'

'Who is she? A mistress?'

Aset answered the questions with increasing reluctance. 'The mistress. If she would accept him he would divorce his wife and take her.'

'Is she married?'

'She is divorced, or widowed. I do not know and I have not asked. He doesn't like to discuss her.'

'Have you met her?'

'No. I have seen her.' An edge of resentment seemed to be in Aset's voice, but Huy did not comment on it.

'What does she do?'

'I do not know. She has money. Perhaps there was a settlement, or an inheritance. She lives in the southeastern quarter.'

Huy spread his hands. 'And what has this to do with Rekhmire?'

Aset looked at him directly with her dark, dazzling eyes. 'Mutnefert is his mistress. His recognised mistress.'

Huy stood up. 'Does he know she has another lover?'

'Does he know about Amotju, you mean? He may have an idea. She is an independent creature. She may have other lovers too.' Again there was the note of resentment.

'Do you disapprove of her?'

'I have nothing to say. Amotju can do as he pleases.'

'Is Rekhmire jealous?'

'You have met him. What he owns, people or goods, he must possess utterly.'

'Then she doesn't sound ideal for him.'

'She represents a challenge. There. Now I have told you everything. You have no need to ask Amotju.' She said this almost bitterly, in a flat voice, as if she had betrayed her brother.

Huy turned to her. 'There was no reason for him to keep this from me. Why do you think he did?'

'He may not have wanted her involved. He is not in command of his heart. She has it.'

'And is that the real reason he wants Rekhmire brought down?'

Aset was silent for a moment. Then she turned her dark eyes on him again. 'We have talked enough about her.' She knelt up in bed and let the sheet fall. 'Come here.'

Huy awoke to the sound of someone hammering on the gate. Then running feet, as people went to open it. Hasty, breathless words he couldn't catch, followed by a muffled conversation, which from its tone was urgent. Aset had already risen, and, drawing a pale blue robe around her, she made for the door. Huy heard her voice raised above the others; a terse exchange of questions and answers. Somebody told to wait. In another minute she was back with him.

'Amotju has gone.'

'Gone?'

'He has disappeared.'

The courtyard of Amotju's house was surrounded by a lime-stone colonnade, and the ground itself was paved in pure white. A fishpool in the centre was fed by a hidden under-ground stream, and a vine trained overhead provided a delicious green shade. Huy sat on a bench carved with a design of birds in a fig tree, impatiently waiting for Amotju's wife to put in an appearance. At last a rustling of clothes made him turn and rise.

It had been a long time since Huy had seen Taheb, but the years had not changed her. She was tall and slim—almost gaunt, as she had always been, and it was only when you were close to her that you saw that the tautness had gone out of her skin, and the little bitter lines around the corners of her mouth became visible under her make-up. Her movements and her behaviour were as they had always been—impeccable and measured. Not one fold of her dress was out of place, and from her manner Huy might have thought that her husband's disappearance was no more than a minor irritation—a slight discrepancy in the accounts; something to be ironed out. She wore a light brown wig with blonde plaits figured into it, to go with her light hazel eyes, which now stared at him unblinkingly, without expression or enthusiasm. Huy recalled that anyone who had had a claim on Amotju's affection, male or female, had always been regarded by Taheb as a potential and unwelcome rival. Too frozen to be able to express the love she felt for him, she had resented anyone with a natural and spontaneous warmth to match his own.

'Huy. Amotju did not tell me you were here again.'

'I have only been back a short time.'

'And are you staying?'

'That depends on work.'

She sat down, but did not motion him to do the same. Nor did she offer him anything.

'What can I do for you?'

'I am trying to find Amotju.'

'There is no need for you to trouble yourself. Our people are making enquiries, and if need be we will take it to the police.'

'What do you think has happened?'

'Who can say? We are hoping it is not a kidnap for ransom. Amotju is a rich man.' This was spoken as a challenge. The marriage had been made to unite fortunes; Huy thought it unlikely that Amotju, however great his passion for Mutnefert, would abandon what he had gained through it, as long as Taheb was prepared to go along with a sexless marriage. They had their children, after all; the succession had been assured. There only remained the status quo to maintain.

'Did he have any enemies?'

'We all have enemies.' What business is it of yours, said her eyes, though they refused to meet his, hovering somewhere at the level of his forehead. Huy wondered how much she resented his presence. If Amotju had not told her that his old friend was back in the Southern Capital, did she suspect a reason she was being kept from knowing? A complicity for her to envy?

Huy tried to keep the conversation faltering along for some time longer, in order to introduce more questions; but he soon saw that Taheb had reached the end of her patience and wanted him to go. Besides, the questions that he needed answering were, he knew, ones that he could hardly put to her under the circumstances. Where had Amotju been last night, if he was not at home? And if he had been, at what time before dawn had he left? And to go where?

'You don't think this has anything to do with the attack on *Glory-of-Ra*?' he asked her, nevertheless.

She gave him a blank stare. 'Why should it be? An enquiry is in train. That is only natural. Why should kidnapping Amotju stop it?'

'You mentioned ransom.'

'The risk is there.' She had had enough. She rose. 'Forgive me, Huy; you were my husband's friend, not mine. I do not welcome former officials of the old regime into my house, nor can I see how our affairs can be any business of yours. I am not certain what prompts all these questions of yours, beyond, I hope, concern for the safety of your friend. But I do not know you well enough to take you into my confidence, nor do I intend to.'

Already missing Aset's mercurial warmth, Huy, told off for a busybody, left. He rolled the idea around in his head that if Amotju were to die, his fleet would go to his oldest son, now not much younger than the new pharaoh; but until his majority it would be run by Taheb. And if Taheb remarried...He was suddenly very curious to look at the company's papers and especially the indentures drawn up between Taheb and Amotju, but now that would have to wait. He made his way back across the city to talk to the other woman in his friend's life.

The contrast in the two houses could not have been greater. Where all at Amotju's had been cool white stone, here at Mutnefert's house one felt embraced by a warm, untidy richness. Even the courtyard was spread with rugs which Huy recognised as coming from far to the northeast, with their rich red and indigo dyes, and their curious, subtle, alien designs. Once, far to the south, he had seen elephants, and it seemed to him that Egyptian art was like those great grey beasts; monumental and open. But here, the art reminded him of swift, small, darting animals: ones that would dwell in caves and under shelves of rock. Many colours danced before his eyes, dark and suggestive.

She welcomed him in an inner room whose furniture was draped heavily in the fabrics of Rettenu and Mitanni, while the walls were hung with a lighter material which shimmered, and which was woven in a pattern wholly unfamiliar to Huy. A servant brought in figs and dates on a tray-table, and he was offered black and red beer, and the flame-liquor. Mutnefert sat opposite him on a couch, reclining against cushions, her feet drawn up under her. A tiny monkey with a bare red face and a ruff of bright yellow fur crouched on her knee, and she stroked it idly.

'I am pleased to meet you at last; though sad at the circumstances. Amotju has spoken of you often.'

'Then I must try not to disappoint.' Huy was partly charmed, and partly cautious. He did his best to conceal his surprise that Amotju had mentioned him to his mistress, and wondered what he had said.

'He told me that you come from the City of the Horizon,' continued Mutnefert, as if thought-reading. 'That must be a sad place now.'

Huy tried to read distress or anxiety in the direct gaze of this woman; but she was too sophisticated to let her guard drop until she had sized him up, which was surely what she was doing through the veil of conversation. He found himself thinking of the proposition ascribed to the ancient philosopher Imhotep, that in any relationship one of the couple loves more than the other: that there is consequently a lover and a beloved, that each of us is naturally one or the other, and must find our counterpart. He imagined that Mutnefert was a taker, and realised with surprise that Taheb was a giver. But which did Amotju really need?

He accepted some red beer; he certainly didn't want anything stronger, and ate a little bread and figs.

'May I ask you some questions about Amotju? I am trying to find out what has happened to him.'

'You can ask me anything you like; but don't you think everyone is getting a little excited a little too early?'

'What do you mean?'

'He might have gone off—on his own account. I don't know.'

Huy wondered at this gipsyish way of thinking, and wasn't sure that he didn't admire it. 'I think it is unlikely that he would have told no one. His body-servants are very concerned.'

'I'm not surprised; but they mustn't blame themselves. Amotju came here alone last night.'

That at least answered the first question. 'Does he always come alone when he visits you?'

'I don't know. I don't ask him. But I shouldn't think so. Last night's visit was—unplanned.'

Huy hesitated, wondering how to ask his next: 'Wasn't that—a risk?'

She looked at him levelly, no doubt wondering how much he knew. 'Amotju was very careful normally. He needed to talk.'

'About the attack on *Glory-of-Ra*?'

'Yes.'

'Was he distressed?'

'He felt that the gods were against him. He wouldn't say why.'

'What did you say?'

'I told him not to be silly.' She smiled, but the smile was a worried one. 'When he left, I thought he was going home.

Home,' she repeated, a little sadly. 'Do you know, we have never spent a complete night together.'

'When did he leave?' Huy, picking up some of her sadness, was embarrassed.

She sighed, sitting up and placing the monkey on the couch next to her. It responded to this treatment with an irritable little chirrup, and looked up at her reproachfully before scampering up the cushions stacked behind her and then dropping to its stomach at the top of the heap.

'He came late; we had a little to eat, he drank too much wine. Then we went to bed, and he lay in my arms and talked. About very little, really. Then he slept. I think he left two hours before dawn, but it might have been earlier still. I cannot count the hours at night.'

As Huy was leaving she stopped him. 'Amotju told me about you. That you cannot work as a scribe any more.'

'That is true, alas.'

She smiled again, more mischievously this time: 'Are you training yourself to be a crime-solver, then?'

'Why do you ask?'

'Because of the way you put questions. Like a senior Medjay. Only possibly more intelligently. I'll have to watch my step with you.'

Huy smiled back. 'No, that is not my ambition. I want to be a scribe again, and live quietly.'

The days that followed brought no news, though the city buzzed with rumour. Amotju had been seen in the Northern Capital; in the Delta; far upriver at Napata. A holy man reported meeting his *Khou*-spirit, who described where the body was to be found; but a search revealed nothing. Ani, as he recovered from his wound, directed those of Amotju's sailors who were in port to make what enquiries they could, but no one remembered seeing Amotju board a barge bound upriver or down, and no ferryman had taken him across the River to the Valley. 'Unless he'd disguised himself,' said Ani. But there seemed to be no reason for Amotju to want to disappear.

On the eighth day a runner brought Aset a letter. Opening it and reading it in the garden, she looked grave.

'It is from Taheb,' she said, looking across at Huy. 'She wants to meet me with the scribes to discuss the future of the fleet.'

'She cannot think he is dead yet?'

'She may not think it; but perhaps she desires it.'

Huy could not believe that either. But in any case the meeting never took place. Later that same day a party of tomb workers found Amotju wandering along the shore of the west bank. He was exhausted and starving. His fine clothes were in rags, and he hardly seemed to know where he was. For a long time he would not speak, though he allowed himself to be washed, tended and dressed. Taheb came into her own, becoming doctor, nurse and mother to him, allowing herself only the minimum of sleep in order to look after him properly.

To Huy, this seemed odd behaviour in someone who only a day earlier had seemed to be anticipating her husband's death before anyone else had begun to give up hope, but he accepted it gratefully, as she unbent sufficiently to allow him to visit the house at any time, though not to ask Amotju questions, or stay long.

For a time, they feared that he had suffered a loss of memory so total that it had not only deprived him of his past, but robbed him of the power of speech. Mutnefert, unable to see him at all, was frantic—a reaction which Huy found almost as surprising as Taheb's, for he had thought Mutnefert a woman well in control of her feelings. He relayed news to her as often as he could, to Aset's disgust; but there was little fresh he could say with each succeeding visit, and nothing good.

Then, minute signs began to appear that Amotju would

emerge from the state of deep shock they had found him in. First of all, recognition came back into his eyes—of where he was, then of whom he was with. Not long after that, his lips began to move as he strained towards forming words. This took a lot longer, but the desire to talk was strong within him, and he struggled until he succeeded. Thereafter, his progress was quick, though his manner remained reserved, and he kept his eyes down when talking to people, unwilling to meet their gaze.

To Taheb's evident annoyance, the person he most urgently wanted to see was Huy. Summoned to the house, he first had to run the gauntlet of his friend's wife, who issued a list of precautions and conditions worthy of a provincial administrator before allowing him into a small inner courtyard. Even then, she left him with as much reluctance as suspicion.

He found himself in a space barely larger than an arbour. The walls here were painted with vigorous, highly coloured designs of ducks flying above lotus groves, of sportsmen hunting water birds with throwing-sticks in the marshes, and of oxen ploughing by the River. The court was dominated by an ancient fig tree which cast its shade over everything, plunging the area into semi-gloom. Amotju sat on a long, low couch spread with gazelle hide, supported by a large bolster. He beckoned Huy over with a listless smile.

'My friend...'

Huy grasped his wrist in greeting, appalled to see how thin it had become. The skin on the backs of his hands was badly broken and scabbed.

'How are you?'

'I cannot believe I am here.'

'You have had a terrible experience.'

'Yes, it was terrible. It brought me to the brink of death.'

'What happened?'

Amotju's face contracted in pain. 'I cannot talk about that! Not now! Not yet!'

Huy was surprised and concerned at the violence of his

emotion. 'I am sorry. I did not mean to distress you.'

'It's all right. Naturally you would want to know.' Amotju relaxed slightly.

Huy said, more gently, 'Can you at least tell me the sequence of events...where you were?'

Amotju looked at him beseechingly. 'If I told you, I am not sure that you would believe me. I do not know if I can face the memory myself yet.'

'Please trust me. Perhaps if you share it...'

His friend's eyes took on a haunted look, as if he expected something to spring at him from the shadows in the corners of the courtyard. He pulled Huy to him, so close that their foreheads touched, and spoke in a voice that was barely audible: 'I have not been to the brink of death, but beyond it.' His eyes met Huy's, imploring him to believe. 'Do not ask me to say any more now. But that is the extent of what has happened.'

Amotju sank back, exhausted, and closed his eyes. Huy watched him for a moment, sitting on the edge of the couch, and then thinking him asleep, started to rise softly. In a moment Amotju was awake, clutching his arm.

'You must do nothing more in pursuit of Rekhmire!'

'What?'

'Nothing! Do you hear me?'

'We will talk. But I must find out who has done this to you.'

'I have received a warning from the gods.'

'Which gods?'

Amotju seemed to be on the point of answering, his heart struggling to give his tongue speech.

'Huy!' Taheb's curt voice, calling him from the entrance to the courtyard. Amotju sank back, his battered hands losing their grip on Huy's arm, where the fingers had left red marks. Huy rose gently, biting back his irritation at Taheb's untimely interruption, and turned to meet her.

'He has had enough,' she said more softly, leading him away and through into the larger quadrangle where they had first met. 'He gets upset very quickly, very easily. What did he tell you?' They passed a house-servant carrying a jug of water, going to tend his master.

'Nothing.'

Taheb looked at him in a way which might have been sceptical, but she indicated a chair, and asked him if he would like bread and wine. This was very different treatment from before, but Huy did not allow his face to betray any of his thoughts. They sat in silence while the food and drink were brought.

'How did he seem to you?' asked Taheb after they had drunk.

'Frightened.'

'Yes. He has been given some terrible shock.'

'Deliberately?'

'What do you think?'

'What has he told you?'

She sighed. 'He says he remembers nothing of what happened—only the fear stays in his memory. But he has asked me to take no action, to let him recover and to forget the whole thing.'

'And will you?'

'I cannot.' She looked at him directly, 'I will not disguise from you the fact that Amotju and I have had...our difficulties. No doubt you know already. It is the kind of thing friends discuss,' she added, with a trace of her customary bitterness and envy. 'But this has made me realise that I cannot abandon him; I seek an answer and I seek revenge. This was a cowardly act.'

'What do you think happened?'

'The doctors found from his faeces that he had been drugged...or poisoned.'

'So it was deliberate.'

'You never thought otherwise for a moment.'

He looked at her and found his gaze coolly and firmly returned.

'Do you suspect me?' she asked. 'Do you think I would be driven to anything so vulgar or so desperate to frighten him off seeing that Mitannite woman?'

So she did know about Mutnefert. Well, it was not surprising. Amotju was not a naturally duplicitous man, and he had never been able to wear two faces effectively. Huy drank some wine. Dakhla this time. Amotju evidently stocked nothing but the best.

'What do you want me to do?'

She smiled; Huy could hardly believe it. 'I should have believed Amotju when he told me you were clever.'

Huy thought, you look at me and you see a stocky little clerk without much money, who has lost his wife and who was foolish enough to have come unstuck when Akhenaten's ship went down. But maybe you're learning.

'I want you to help me find out who is behind this.'

'He asked me to drop everything.'

'And will you?'

Huy wondered if she knew about the original threat, the ichneumon symbolically robbed of its life and the strength of its right arm after death. It seemed unlikely that Amotju would have told her about it. He also wondered how politically ambitious she was, through her husband. He noticed that she had not mentioned Rekhmire. It was difficult, not knowing how far she was in Amotju's confidence, and not knowing how sure she was of keeping him. Aset had said he would leave her for Mutnefert.

'I think I would like to find out the truth. I do not like mysteries.'

'Some things are hidden from us for ever by the gods.'

'There is very little that determination cannot uncover.'

After this short, formal exchange that signalled their agreement, they smiled at each other cautiously. Taheb raised her cup and drank.

Glory-of-Ra had been floated off the sandbank and completed her journey to the port of the Southern Capital with what was left of her cargo. There she was unloaded and overhauled, the planking damaged in the battle replaced, and the bloodstains scoured from her decks. Ani had been able to supervise most of this. Gradually getting used to his new cedarwood leg, with its linen cushion and leather straps, he now rested on his single crutch to ease the soreness he still felt in his stump, and let his eyes run over the lines of his ship with satisfaction. Mobile again, and assured of his old command back, he had spent the preceding days recruiting a fresh crew. Soon he might be sailing up to the Northern Capital. *Glory-of-Ra* was possibly to be consort to *Splendour-of-Amun* as escorts to Nebkheprure Tutankhamun as he sailed south to take up his new residence.

Ani felt a glow of satisfaction. After the uncertainties and vicissitudes of the last decade and a half, the world would be right again. There was only one loose end to be tidied up before he could settle with a clear mind to his work once more, and that was the matter of justice—or vengeance. Ani did not particularly care which motivated him more: the men who had robbed him of his ship, slaughtered his crew, and seen him mutilated by the crocodiles, had to be found.

The rule of law had declined rapidly on the upper reaches of the River during the last two reigns, and pirates, unknown in Ani's youth, during the rule of Amenophis III, had emerged in their hundreds from the ranks of disaffected or cashiered sailors, deserters from the navy, and freelance captains who looked for a quick and high profit from crime. Ani knew that there would be no question of bringing all the individuals involved to justice, though through passing the word among his network of contacts up and down the River he had the satisfaction of knowing that five of them had had their throats cut. Solidarity amongst the honest sailors on the River had less to do with sentiment than insurance; and their justice was swifter and a good deal more conclusive than that meted out by the courts.

Ani's thoughts, however, were focused on the Medjay officer who had sat watching as his men were slaughtered. He must have been very cocksure to show himself like that; though in truth the battle had been all but over when he had appeared. The problem was that you did not trace a Medjay, still less an officer, through unofficial channels; and even if you were able to do that, there would be little or no chance of administering the rough justice Ani had seen dealt out to his other enemies. That morning, however, he had received news which gave him some cause to celebrate. Three of the peasant farmers who had rescued him had also seen the Medjays, and as Ani had added judicious bribes of his own to the reward paid by Amotju, these men had agreed to testify with him in any trial.

All that had remained was to track down the Medjay, and that had turned out to be easier than Ani had expected. That morning he had had confirmation that the man's name was Intef; he had recently been appointed to a post at Esna.

'The arrogance of the man is unbelievable,' he told Huy when he passed on the information. 'But of course someone like him regards peasant farmers as barely above the animals in the fields, and he thought that we were all killed.'

'I don't know if we can get him.'

'Of course we can get him. Horemheb is determined to put a stop to the crime that's developed in the country. Especially down here, where it's so bad people can't even cross the port area in the capital at night.'

'He won't like it if one of his own men is involved. Whoever brings the charge may win, but he won't be popular.'

'I'll take that risk,' said Ani, evenly. 'If I don't have a legitimate complaint, who has?'

'But what case do you have?'

'They were so close to us. They could have saved us!'

'That proves nothing.'

'It proves they weren't doing their duty!'

'They might have felt it imprudent to intervene. You know the way they think.'

Ani grimaced in irritation.

'I know you don't like it; but we have to think strategically, within the law,' said Huy.

'If I'd thought you were going to turn out to be such a cold fish, I wouldn't have come to you with this. I thought Amotju was your friend.'

'Stirring up the Medjays against him won't help.'

'So what are you saying?'

'That we need concrete proof.'

'You've got four witnesses!'

'Proof that he was in on the attack.'

Ani was about to reply; then he relaxed, as if something had occurred to him. He grinned. 'You'll get your proof,' he said.

Three days later, Intef was arrested. A chest of gold ingots bearing Amotju's stamp had been found under the floor of his stable.

'I don't believe that anyone could be that stupid,' said Aset, when Huy told her.

'It might just have been that he felt absolutely sure of himself,' Huy said. 'Arrogance, but not stupidity.'

'What's the difference?'

'There will be a trial.'

'When?'

'Immediately. Horemheb is very displeased. He wants it all cleared up and forgotten as soon as possible. At the same time, he's going to make an example of this man.'

'If he's guilty.'

'Three men saw him, and Ani. Now there's the gold.'

'Have you talked to Ani about this?'

'Of course.'

'What does he say?'

'That the gods answered his prayers.'

'And do you believe him?'

Huy looked at her. He had already checked the dockets itemising the gold offloaded from *Glory-of-Ra* at the port, against the boxes of rough ingots and nuggets now in Amotju's strongrooms, and there was no discrepancy.

'No,' he said. 'Any more than I believe that Intef was behind it, though he was almost certainly part of it.'

The trial was held at Esna and did not take long. The young officer protested his innocence but there was no denying the damning evidence, and the matter had to be hurried through. The dry season was coming to an end, and people were preoccupied with the coming floods, as Hapy, the breasted god, spread the rich water of the River wide over the thirsty land. Then the king would come to the Southern Capital. On a dawn when the fresh north wind was blowing, Intef was taken down to the water's edge, where a stake, two paces long and a hand's-breadth across, had been jammed firmly between rocks, the roughly sharpened end pointing to the sky. They stripped him, raised him up, inserted the point of the stake in his anus, and impaled him. There was not a great crowd. People were too busy preparing for the floods. Because he was a Medjay, the jailers had seen to it that he had had too much fig liquor to drink on his last night on earth. Thus it was, that he was barely conscious until the pain hit him; and then he was not conscious any more, ever.

As he had told Taheb, Huy did not like mysteries. They were untidy, in the same way that Intef's death was untidy. It was supposed to solve problems, tie up a number of loose ends, and it had achieved neither aim, except for the purpose of official records. But whom had Intef been working with? Would they be likely to avenge him? Executing him might have a discouraging effect on other Medjays wanting to take a short cut to fortune, but Huy was simply frustrated that the man had been killed before he had had a chance to talk to him. Offering him clemency in exchange for information was a new idea, and one which would probably not have appealed to Horemheb; still, it was a pity that there had not been an opportunity for the attempt.

But his interest in Intef would draw attention to him which he would soon find unwelcome.

Aset had managed to get him an introduction through her brother's contacts to the clerk who had responsibility for checking the offloading of the remaining part of *Glory-of-Ra's* cargo, the man whose paperwork Huy had already had a chance of inspecting.

The clerk was not too pleased to see Huy again. He was the model of clerical self-regard, and might have stepped straight out of those pages of *The Miscellanies* that deal with scribes, thought Huy. Tall and immaculate, except for his finger-ends, which bore carefully neglected inkstains to underline the status of his profession, the man had all the marks of the ambitious junior who wants to appear more important than he really is. In contrast to the battered palette which Huy no longer carried, this clerk's was brand-new. It was made of sycamore wood inlaid with ebony, with a long indentation scooped down the middle to hold the (in this case) perfectly straight rush brushes. Above this notch six circular holes were carved into the wood, each holding a cake of pressed ink powder, four black and two red. At his belt, the clerk carried two neat leather pouches, with further supplies of ink powder. The man looked so refined that Huy wondered if he used only water or sometimes spittle to moisten the ink, and whether he lowered himself to chew the ends of his own rushes, to split the fibres and create the brush.

'Greetings, Pemou,' said Huy, as he entered the man's room near the quay.

'Is anything amiss?' Pemou wanted to know immediately. He knew all about Huy and was wary, but at the same time didn't want to alienate the boss's friend.

'No.'

'The documents you saw were in order, I hope?'

'Perfectly.'

Pemou was still worried. He nibbled the end of one of his pens, and, reaching across his low desk, adjusted one or two of the items on it: a small tortoiseshell containing water, and a roll of leather which he used as a writing surface. Seeing these familiar objects, Huy felt a pang of envy and of nostalgia. He wondered if he would ever be allowed to use them again. He noticed that Pemou even wore a clay talisman of Thoth, the god of writing, around his neck. This man was a copybook scribe.

'If nothing's amiss, what can I do for you?'

Huy wondered whether the nervousness simply sprang from Pemou's dislike at having to deal with this dubious character. A former resident of Akhetaten, the City of the Horizon, would not be desirable company for an ambitious man, no matter how small fry.

'I'd just like to ask you one or two questions which have occurred to me since I read the cargo lists.'

Pemou looked around the empty room, as if expecting to

surprise an eavesdropper lurking in a corner.

'Have you permission to be here?'

Huy looked into the shifty eyes but failed to hold them. What was the man thinking? He knew that, if out of danger, Amotju was certainly nowhere near recovered. Was the man considering that for the time being, at least, he should switch his loyalty to the acting-manager, Taheb?

'Not written down.'

'There should be something—'

'Come on!' Huy almost went on to say, 'We're colleagues.' But he bit the words back; he no longer had the right to make that claim. 'This has absolutely nothing to do with your accounts of the cargo,' Huy continued, carefully, he hoped. He had no wish to make enemies where there was no need.

'I should think not! If I thought for a moment that you doubted—'

Huy held up a hand to soothe him. 'I want to know who saw the cargo before you did.'

Pemou nibbled his pen, looking down.

'Did anyone?'

A quick look up. 'Where is all this leading?'

'Nowhere. It's simply a question of confirming that no one tampered with the cargo after you'd made the inventory.'

'That man Intef was guilty!' Pemou spat suddenly. 'What's the world coming to, when the police turn to crime? We have to be protected against such people!'

'That isn't an issue at all,' lied Huy. 'Amotju simply wants me to confirm that no one else took advantage of the confusion to help themselves to some of what was left on board. And he has complete faith in your probity, or he wouldn't have sent me to ask you about it directly like this.'

Huy hoped that no one would check on this string of lies, but he could see already that it had done the trick. The combination of Amotju's name mentioned with authority, and the judicious praise of himself, apparently reflecting Amotju's honest opinion of him, made Pemou positively swell with pride. He stood up importantly, trying not to smile, and adjusted the folds of his kilt, faultlessly tucked beneath a nascent potbelly, round and smooth as an earthenware jar.

'Let me see...' But Huy knew that this wasn't playing for time; this was making the most of the importance of the moment.

'Of course there was the skeleton crew which went down to collect the barge, but they were under strict supervision from the moment they left here until the moment they brought *Glory-of-Ra* back. I made the inventory almost immediately...I know! Ani, the old captain. He went aboard almost as soon as she docked and the crew had disembarked. I remember because I was working late, as I frequently do.' He paused to let this facet of his diligence sparkle for a moment. 'And I noticed them pass.'

'Them?'

'Yes. I knew it was Ani because of the crutch, of course. He still had quite a lot of difficulty in walking. It's remarkable how quickly— '

'Who was with him?' Huy tried to continue to sound politely interested, and to keep the excitement out of his voice.

'Two body-servants. Big men.'

'Did you notice from which household?'

Pemou looked surprised: 'Why, Amotju's.'

Huy breathed deeply: 'And did you see them again?' 'No. They must have still been on the boat when I left. It was very late.'

'Wasn't a watchman posted?'

'Yes, but why should he have had any reason to—'

'Where is he now?'

Pemou looked uncomfortable. 'The fact is—'

'Yes?'

Pemou looked like a child whose sandcastle on the banks of the River had just been flattened by the tread of a clumsy heifer. 'He disappeared soon afterwards. Hasn't been seen since, in fact. He hadn't been with us long, in any case, and we just thought he'd gone after a better job elsewhere.'

Huy looked thunderous. 'Was Amotju informed of this?'

Pemou trembled. 'I don't know...On account of his disappearance—Amotju's, I mean and his illness...In any case, the watchman wasn't my responsibility, or something would certainly have been reported.'

Huy left him considering means of rebuilding his sandcastle.

Although it was still early in the new season, the waters of the River were already noticeably higher and the sides of the ships were beginning to rise like wooden walls along the edges of the quays. The sun seemed to take longer in his daily journey from birth to death, and to hover at his central station high in the sky above their heads for what seemed an interminable time. Many now dispensed with their wigs in the daytime, wearing a white linen headdress instead, and no women of any quality were to be seen in the streets before evening. The city lay in torpor, like a ghost town. The fields, too, lay empty, waiting to be flooded by Hapy, bringing his riches of silt and water to the parched soil; and everyone moved to the high ground. Soon, the Dog Star would rise, and the new year would begin. Huy disliked the summer, and looked forward to the activity and relative coolness of Peret, the season of Coming Forth.

He found Ani aboard ship. The *Glory-of-Ra* was almost completely restored, owing to the number of men who could at present be drafted from labouring on the land to shipbuilding. It was the tenth day, the last day of the week, and work was slackening off in preparation for the Day of Rest. Huy was glad to have found Ani, and found him alone.

Ani was expansive, showed Huy proudly round the barge, poured wine, and would not be hurried. He behaved like a man in a very secure position, and through his conversation wove a thread which warned Huy that his own status in Amotju's household was by no means as certain. Huy noticed that the wine was from Dakhla. Not the sort you'd expect a bargemaster to serve. He drank sparingly. Ani noticed this, but did not stint himself.

'Well, you'd better ask me what you came to ask me,' he said, finally, when he could procrastinate no more.

'I want to know what you thought of Intef.'

Ani paused before replying. 'It was good to see him squirm at his trial.'

'Do you think it was a fair trial?'

'Thirty of my men drowned or were killed. We only recovered five to bury. I saw him on the bank, watching.'

'He wasn't alone.'

A gesture of impatience. 'His men were nothing! Instruments! They won't be clever enough to escape the investigation Horemheb's set up.'

That was true. Three other policemen had been brought to trial since Intef's execution. Two had been found guilty, and had had their noses and right hands cut off. The body of Intef still hung on its stake. The rising waters of the River had reached his waist, and soon the crocodiles would finish him.

'I know what you went through.'

'Do you, now?' Ani's voice was heavy with sarcasm. Bloody little pernickety scribe, he was really saying. What do you know?

'Don't you worry that Intef's friends won't avenge him?'

'Against whom? The law? He had a fair trial. If he was stupid enough to hide booty in his own stables…'

'Then he'd also have been stupid enough to tell someone close. Do you think he was that stupid?'

'What are you saying?'

'How did you get the gold into his house?'

There was a pause; then Ani spread his hands. 'Trade secret.'

'It can't be hard to get a light boat up to Esna, and there'd be enough willing hands to help, if they knew the man had stood by and let sailors die.'

'You said yourself Intef was guilty. There were so many witnesses, after all. You said all that was needed was conclusive proof, to clinch it. I provided that. It was just a matter of giving justice a helping hand.'

Huy sighed inwardly. The milk was spilt, and Intef was gone.

'The man had it coming. How many other attacks like that do you think he'd planned?' Ani went on, justifying himself and beginning to bluster. Huy toyed with the idea of suggesting to him that Intef hadn't been the mastermind, that there was probably someone else whom he might have led them to; but there seemed to be no point.

'That's the trouble with you people,' Ani was saying. 'You want to do everything by the book. Well, thank the gods that there's still room for some natural justice. I couldn't have borne to see a man like him go free.'

'Can't you just tell me who helped you?'

'Why do you want to know?'

'I'm curious.'

'That's not a good enough reason.'

'Tell me anyway. Did Amotju?'

'No,' said Ani, knowing that Huy could check such a thing, not knowing that Amotju had effectively dispensed with Huy's services. 'But friends. Powerful friends.' There was more than a note of warning in his voice as he spoke.

Huy gave up. This was an alley with a wall across the end. He would have to retrace his steps.

The gangplank ran almost horizontally from deck to quay, so high had the River now risen, and Huy crossed it thoughtfully after he had bidden Ani an uneasy farewell. He was fond of the captain, and entirely sympathised with his motives, though he would never have followed the same course of action.

He smiled inwardly at himself. He had never seen himself as a man of action at all, rather one who preferred safety, sensual pleasures and the maintenance of a status quo—as long as it was one with which he could square his conscience. And yet here he was, rummaging in other people's lives, maybe attracting enemies of his own who were as yet perfect strangers to him.

Behind him, the sun nudged the rim of the horizon, and the glittering on the River turned first golden, then copper, then red. He looked at the stones ahead of him, golden too, and at his shadow, lengthening with every step he took, its jagged outline faithfully reflecting each ripple and minor gulley of stone his movement threw it across. He imagined another kind of quiet life: the one the farmers still had, but which he feared the politicians and the power-hungry had cast away for ever as they had discovered the strength of their own personalities. The farmers were still the possessions of the pharaoh—of the sun and of the River; they had no time for more than their work, no desire beyond their food and their lovemaking, and above all, no notion of themselves as individuals, which, Huy was beginning to realise, was the root of unhappiness. When had feeling emerged from soothing numbness? Had it been there when Menes united the Black Land, two thousand years earlier?

But even the farmers were not immune from fear, and Huy had heard of murders among them.

As evening brought respite from the heat of the day, so people began to spill on to the streets, and shops and booths opened. Making his way back to Aset's, Huy felt more comfortable in the midst of the throng. Just having people around kept gloomier thoughts at bay. Practically, too, it was easier to ensure one's anonymity in a crowd.

On the other hand, it was far more difficult to ascertain whether or not one was being followed, and Huy had little experience in such matters, allowing himself to be guided by instinct and the strong motivation that Aset should be protected from any evil aimed at him, or likely to befall him. This time his guides let him down.

He had turned down an alley between the blank walls of two large houses, which linked two main streets. It was a long alley and it incorporated two sharp bends. Turning the corner of one of these, he was confronted by three men, all southerners, in Medjay kilts, blocking his path.

'Huy, the former scribe?'

'You know I am.'

'Come with us.' The officer who spoke stood on the left of the trio. He had a quiet, almost tired voice, but it carried an edge which expected no argument. Huy glanced from one to the other of the Medjays. They seemed to be carrying no weapons, but to run or to fight would be useless. Huy bowed his head. The first man turned on his heel without another word and started to walk away. Huy fell into step behind, as the other two took up their positions after him. The little procession didn't have far to go. They had almost reached the main street when they stopped at a small archway Huy had not noticed before. He was ushered through it, and then they took hold of his arms and marched him down a corridor to the left, finally pushing him into a surprisingly large room. It had high windows and its walls were of plain mud-brick. It was oppressively hot. The rough wooden door was closed behind him, and a bolt slotted across the outside.

Huy sat down on a clay bench built into the wall and looked at the windows. You could reach them if you stretched up fully, but even if you could pull yourself up to them, they would be too small to climb through—and even then there was no guarantee that they didn't give on to an internal courtyard.

Time passed in utter silence. Wiping the sweat from his shoulders, Huy paced the room. He knew they were leaving him to stew, but that knowledge didn't help much. Sooner or later, he told himself, they would come and deal with him. That knowledge didn't help much either.

Finally there was a sound of heavy footfalls in the corridor outside. He tried to deduce the number of people from the sound, but it was impossible because of the deadening effect of the mud-brick. He stood well back from the door and faced it as he heard the bolt drawn.

Two soldiers entered the room quickly, and one of them hit Huy with the thick stick he was carrying, hard enough to make him double up and sink to his knees, winded. In the couple of seconds it took him for his vision to clear he felt a cool breeze and smelt the unmistakable smells of fresh linen and lotus blooms—the smells of power and wealth. Without raising his eyes he could see the golden hem of a long blue kilt, above strong, tanned feet in leather sandals fastened with gold studs. The feet were clean and well cared for, but their soles were hard and their insteps were a lattice of knotted veins. The cool breeze had been caused by their owner's vigorous entry to the room.

Huy raised his eyes further and quickly, until he found himself looking into a lean, hard face with thin lips and a curved nose above which two piercing black-brown eyes, like a hawk's, burnt down at him. The eyes met his for an instant before one of the soldiers forced his head down and he was staring at the red baked-mud floor. But his heart was racing. General Horemheb!

'I know who you are and what your sentence was, Scribe Huy,' came a hard baritone from somewhere above him. 'I know your involvement in the case of Intef. I know you have sought work of the kind now forbidden you. You seem to think little of the concession made to you by sparing your life. That I continue to spare it is a mark of my gratitude to you for helping bring Intef to justice. But do not make a habit of it. Leave the law to those qualified and sanctioned to carry it out. I am not unmerciful, but if I find you become even the smallest thorn in my side, I will pluck you out and throw you on the fire.'

Huy felt rather than saw the general give a sign with his hand, and each soldier brought his heavy stick down over his bowed back, striking squarely across the kidneys. His breath gone, Huy squirmed on the floor, panicking as he struggled to get his lungs working. His world shrank to the confines of his body, and he was aware of nothing outside it. When, finally, and with a cascading relief, he managed to get air into himself again, and came to his senses, he found himself alone in the room. He couldn't decide whether or not the general's visit had been a dream.

He saw that the door had been left open. Outside, the corridor was deserted. He walked down it confidently, sure that his departure was allowed. He met no one else until he had left the alleyway outside and rejoined the people still walking in the main street outside, though he could tell by the colour of the sky how late it was. Hurrying through the dim light shed by the few shopkeepers' oil-lamps, he made his way up through the city to Aset's house.

She greeted his proposal that he leave with such anger that for a few days he gave in to her persuasion and his own natural disinclination to go. But he could not prevent his heart from brooding on fear for her safety.

'I am all right if you are with me,' she said. 'In any case, if it is Horemheb who knows that you are here, then you are safe too. If he wanted to do you harm, he would do so. Wherever you were, you could not escape him.'

'But if Horemheb knows, others may know too. The number of servants who know already is too high. Such a large number cannot be trusted.'

'You are saying that because you want to go.'

'Believe me, I do not.'

But she continued to sulk until he gave in, and went to soothe her; yet, as hard as he tried, he could not lose himself in her kisses, and she knew it.

'If this is going to sour our lovemaking, then it is better that we part; but I am not going to let you go,' said Aset. 'Not for ever, for I do not really believe that that is what you want.'

'What do you want?'

'To be with you always.'

'Even in the best of worlds I could not ever be your husband,' said Huy. 'Married to me, you would carry the stain that I do. Amotju would not advise you to take such action. Your marriage must benefit your family.'

'Your excuses are as hollow as they sound,' said Aset.

That night, they made love long and lingeringly, gently and cruelly, as the waves of their desire broke over them. In the morning, awakening before dawn, Huy kissed her sleeping face with more tenderness, he thought, than he had ever felt even for Aahmes, even at the height of their love, when he would look down on her sleeping with little Heby next to her. His son would be learning to write by now. He wondered how he was managing, whether his master was as fierce as his own had been; he wondered what Heby looked like. There is an immeasurable difference between three and seven. But now, it seemed to him, he had found someone to fill the void in his heart. If only he could let himself go, and give in to his feelings.

He made his way to his own room. Although it had a bed in it, he used it as an office. He had planned to write down every step in his investigation—but so far he had only succeeded in charting each loose end on a separate sheet of papyrus.

It was still early, and although he could hear movement in the kitchen at the top of the house, muffled and cautious as the baker sought to disturb no one, the rest of the building was wrapped in the profound silence that settles on life when night is at its deepest. Reaching his door, his foot scuffed something small and hard, placed on the floor outside it. He knelt and peered down at it through the semi-gloom, and picking it up found it to be a stone scarab, of the sort on which commemorative inscriptions were incised. He carried it along the short corridor to where an oil-lamp glowed in a recess in the wall. There he turned it over. On its base one hieroglyph was cut: the sign for death.

Suddenly, all the warmth rushed out of him, and the friendly darkness filled with threat. Still clutching the scarab, and taking the oil-lamp with him, he retraced his steps silently and hastily. At the door of his room he hesitated; but then, overcoming his fear, he pushed it open firmly, and entered.

Even by the feeble glimmer the lamp cast on it from a distance, he could see that someone, or something, was lying in the bed. He placed the scarab on a table by the door and moved forward. He was unarmed, but the rigid stillness of whatever it was in the bed told him that it posed no direct threat. At first, the light only allowed him to make out that it was covered by a linen sheet, and that the sheet was marred by an enormous dark stain at its centre. There was a faint smell which made the hair on the back of his neck rise: the odour of long-dead fish and sulphur lingered in the room.

He saw that although the proportions of the thing in the bed were human, the head was not. It was too long. What should have been the nose was pulled forward into a snout, the forehead had been flattened backwards, and the hair and chin had disappeared. There seemed to be no mouth, until he realised that the head was all mouth—huge extended jaws containing...But they contained nothing. And the eyes were sightless holes. Huy saw that this was a crocodile mask, the skin of a dead animal stretched over a light wooden frame. He leant forward cautiously to touch it, then sprang back as it appeared to move; but it was only a trick of the gloom.

He had stumbled and instinctively reached out to steady himself, touching the sheet. It was cold and wet, sticky and wet, and what was under it was cold and soft. Even without the thin light he could have told that it was blood, for the smell of it was strong on his fingers. Hardly believing in the waking nightmare he had walked into, he gingerly took the dry corners of the sheet and pulled it back, having to tug it gently when it stuck. He half knew what to expect, but when he saw it, glistening in the yellow glow of the lamp, his gorge rose and he had to breathe long and slowly to conquer his nausea. A male human corpse which had been flayed. Whoever had done the job was a master, for not a trace of skin remained, even on the penis.

Huy's eyes travelled up the trunk to the grotesque mask, though he already knew who this was. One of the legs ended just below the knee.

'You mustn't tell him,' said Taheb. 'He is making good progress now, and news like this will cause a relapse.'

'He will want to know the reason I am leaving.'

'Will he? You may be surprised.'

'What do you mean?' asked Huy.

'I'll let him tell you.' She looked at him in silence for a moment, then said, 'I'd like to know what progress you have made. If any.'

'I wanted to talk to Intef.'

'What good would that have done?'

'Everything is aimed at Amotju.'

'Nonsense. His father's tomb was only one of many that have been robbed recently. And as for river pirates, they are everywhere.'

'But the robbery of the tomb, the piracy and the abduction, all coming together…'

'Amotju thinks that he was carried off by gods or demons under Rekhmire's control,' said Taheb drily.

'And do you believe that?'

'I must believe my husband's opinion.'

'When I was up at the tomb I was attacked by Set,' said Huy after a moment's hesitation, 'or someone dressed to look like him. Who sent me there? What people are these robbers to go in for amateur theatricals?'

Taheb drew in her breath sharply. 'What you are saying may be blasphemous. We are very well aware of the heresy you took part in; but the old gods are back in their rightful place.'

Huy knew that Taheb was too intelligent to believe any such thing, but dared not say so. 'I do not think I would merit a personal attack from Set.'

'If you think that there is a connection between these three events, and that Rekhmire is behind them, then I look to you to provide proof that we can take to Horemheb. And I expect you to make better progress than you are. You are an intelligent man.'

'I will try,' said Huy, wondering again whether this enigmatic woman wasn't in some way challenging that intelligence; and asking himself what personal political interests lay behind desiring Rekhmire's fall. 'But the manner of Ani's death and the placing of his corpse present such a direct threat to me that I cannot ignore it. I must retreat.'

Taheb pursed her lips. 'Intef's family took revenge. Anyone might have seen you meeting Ani before the trial, and afterwards again. Ani was the principal witness against Intef. Perhaps their revenge just takes the form of killing him in so cruel a way as to scare you off permanently. How did Aset take it?'

'She didn't see the body. I had three of the house-servants clear the room and take away the corpse. But she knows what happened.' It occurred to Huy that his friend's wife was asking too many questions, and he was disinclined to answer more than he had to.

'Trustworthy house-servants?'

'What can they say? Ani had no family, but his friends will be told. As for Intef's family, he too had none that I have been able to trace. He was half Mitannite. Perhaps all his family live far to the north.'

'So who avenged him?'

Huy bowed his head. He was getting tired of questions.

'Perhaps they will have achieved their ends,' said Taheb. 'I can't see you being able to do much from a hiding place. Where will you go?'

'I haven't decided that yet.'

Taheb challenged the lie with her eyes but said nothing. Huy wondered if he had gone too far.

'Although I would like you to continue to work for us, in

the circumstances you will understand that I can only pay you on results,' she said finally. 'And now you had better talk to my husband. He is waiting for you in the inner courtyard. Be careful how you tell him about Ani.'

Amotju sat on a low chair, his feet on a stool, and was in the act of pouring wine when Huy entered the little atrium. As he looked up, Huy could see that, physically at least, he was his old self. But his eyes retained a hooded, haunted look.

'How are you?' Huy clasped his friend's hands and noticed that the skin on their backs was still scarred.

'Well.' replied Amotju, though his voice was strained, even slurred. Huy wondered that Taheb allowed him such free access to wine. As carefully as he could, he gave Amotju the news of Ani's death, skirting around any details that the sick man did not need to know. Amotju took it sombrely.

'He was my best captain.'

'He was certainly loyal.'

'The ships were his whole world. The men were his family. I will see to it that he has a good burial. He will be rewarded in the Fields of Aarru. The embalmers will make him as whole as they can.' A sudden thought struck him. 'They did not take away his heart?'

'No; they had that much mercy.' Huy shuddered at the thought. To take away a person's heart was to deny them life in the hereafter; it was like killing the soul. The dead thus dispossessed were doomed to wander the earth, seeking the opportunity to take the heart of a living man, to make themselves whole again. Not all his years at the enlightened court of the City of the Horizon had quite dispelled the doubt from his mind that still caused him to fear such things, more than the old gods.

When Huy explained that the implied threat to himself made it necessary for him to withdraw for a time, Amotju barely listened. He seemed to remain uninterested even when Huy drew the parallels that suggested themselves between this more brutal warning and the one issued to Amotju himself in the form of the caged ichneumon. Only someone with great skill and power—and, yes, quite possibly the help of demons—would have been able to achieve this.

Amotju heard him out, drinking steadily, then raised a weary hand: 'I understand all that you have said; but it seems that you have not understood me. I no longer wish you to continue with this investigation. You may not be satisfied, but I am. I am satisfied still to have my life and my fortune. You may choose to ignore threats in order to seek out the truth. I am contented now to yield the palm to Rekhmire, if he will leave me in peace.'

'And will you see Mutnefert again—or do you intend to leave her to Rekhmire too?'

Amotju suddenly looked at him with far more of the glint of his old self in his eyes. 'What?'

'Your mistress. Will you give her up to your rival?'

'Who told you this?'

'It might have helped me to know.'

'It had nothing to do with your work.'

'I have seen love undo kings,' said Huy, thinking now, too, of the intense love the old king, Akhenaten, had borne his great queen, Nefertiti. Seven daughters and no son, and still he slept with no one but her.

'Whatever else, I will have nothing more to do with you. There has been nothing but trouble since you arrived, and Rekhmire goes from strength to strength.'

There was enough fight in his friend's voice now to give Huy hope that the battle wasn't over after all. 'So, you are not scared enough to give up your mistress?'

Amotju stood up. 'Get out,' he said. 'Get out now!'

The River was rising faster now, steadily. Every day you could see a difference, and the water was taking on the green colour that heralded the arrival of Hapy with his gifts. Soon, perhaps even before the new king arrived, although people hoped not, because the colour was inauspicious, the water would turn red, taking the tint of the rich earth that came as Hapy's gift from the south, from the upper reaches of the River, which some claimed to have seen, and from the Atbara.

The interview with Amotju determined Huy not to return to the City of the Horizon—which had been his plan. Instead, he would stay. His friend's refusal to continue to investigate what was behind his recent misfortunes made Huy all the more determined to do so, and he had told Amotju that this was his intention before leaving the house. But as he walked through the dusty streets his temper cooled, and he began to consider more soberly what was best to be done.

He would, he argued, have been safer back in the City of the Horizon than if he remained at the Southern Capital; but he would then have been too far for even a hint of unfolding events to reach him. What was more, the threat brought directly into Aset's house made him less rather than more determined to distance himself from her, because he couldn't know what harm might come to her in his absence; and although he doubted the effectiveness of his role as her protector, he knew he could not leave her. He knew, too, though he had striven hard to deny it to himself, that he loved her.

But staying meant taking her into his confidence. For the

time being, Aset would be his eyes and ears. The situation could not last long, though: it would be impossible to keep his presence a secret indefinitely, and his resources were all but spent. Some form of income would have to be sought soon.

At first, Aset, who had been so anxious for him to stay, was worried that by doing so he would put himself in greater danger. He reassured her, and, using the last of the savings he had brought from the City of the Horizon, together with the payment made to him by Amotju, he rented a small, two-roomed house in the crowded poor area of the city close to the harbour. Here, the drifting population of sailors and foreigners from far to the north and the south would provide him with sufficient cover to pass unnoticed. If both Horemheb and Rekhmire thought that he had gone, he could continue his investigation of the priest's affairs without risking his life. He needed to earn the fee Taheb was still offering him, and Ani's murder had robbed him of a friend, redoubling his own desire for justice—and vengeance. The original threats to Amotju, the figure of Set which had attacked him, the recurrent smell of rotting fish and sulphur, the callous theatricality of Ani's death, so clearly related to Intef's execution, were all interlinked—whatever Taheb thought, or wished him to think.

He settled down quickly in his new surroundings, finding comfort in the crowds, and the uncaring bustle. The landlord had barely looked at him, hadn't checked the false name he'd given, and had only flickered into life and taken real care when it came to the down payment of the rent. In the racial melting-pot of the docks, Huy decided further to blur his identity, after a short battle with disgust, by allowing his beard to grow.

Rekhmire looked across the room at her. She was sitting in her usual chair, by the window, her smooth skin vividly lit by the last rays of the sun, as the noise of the street below gradually died away. Evening was giving way to night. She sat quietly, apparently unaware of his presence; but he knew that the act was about to begin, the little play which he had written for them both, and which he enjoyed every time as freshly as if it were the first. It was a scenario in which he could forget that he had a hump on his back and a club foot; deformities which had driven him relentlessly to prove himself in life, to dominate and control other people, and still to seek the approval of parents, now long dead, who had never praised him, but only demanded more.

Mutnefert, he thought, understood him. She even seemed to enjoy the cruelty, to succumb to him just as he wished. Why, then, was he frightened of her? Why did he rein himself in? Was it just that he was afraid of losing her? Looking at her tonight, he almost faced the question he had so long sought to avoid: why was this the only way he could find to approach her—or any woman before her? This little game of domination and subjection they played. He knew that he had never had a conversation with her, and that apart from sex he barely knew her. He had never attempted to probe her thoughts—he had always told himself, if he had given the matter any thought at all, that this was because they did not interest him. Now, despite himself, he found a suspicion creeping into his heart that the real reason was that he was afraid of what he might find out—about her, and about himself.

Another suspicion that had crept in, undermining his usual pugnacious self-confidence, was that he was losing her. Each time they met, she seemed more and more drawn into herself, and there were times when she would not look at him, when it seemed that he might as well not have been there. On these occasions it was necessary to hurt her more; but still there was no reaching her. Rekhmire could not bear to confront the feeling this created in his heart. It was an unfamiliar feeling to him, and one which he could not afford to acknowledge. If he had been forced to give it a name—though he never would—that name would have been desolation. Was, then, the name for the fear of losing her, love? He barely dared acknowledge the half-formation of such questions in his heart. His heart had been used since childhood to seeing attack as the best form of defence, and political power and material advantage as the best bastions against mockery and condescension.

She turned to him now, and he tensed in expectancy, though still she did not appear to see him. She was like a figure in a dream. She stood, and with a languorous slowness, started to undress, her firm brown limbs and broad shoulders emerging from the folds of pristine white linen in a way that was both tantalising and innocent. His eyes embraced the soft curve of her buttocks; his throat became dry; the tips of his teeth tingled. Then their eyes met, as she seemed to notice him for the first time. He read what he wanted to in hers: surprise, and hurt innocence vying with the anticipation of guilty pleasure. She was a good actress. He rose in his turn and grasped the stick by his side.

Afterwards he never lay down beside her. Usually he would leave immediately, for tenderness had no role to play in his impoverished lovemaking. But today he lingered. He knew, of course, that it was all a game, the only real thing being the pain he inflicted on her when he forgot to rein himself in. Now, though, there were these new feelings, and the sense of her remoteness disturbed him. He felt her eyes on him again, but they were different. The eyes of the off-duty actress, uninterested, wanting him to leave, so that she could bathe, change, wash his smell and his memory away until the next time. These things had never disturbed him before, never entered his heart. The question in her eyes was clear to read: 'Why are you still here?' He felt a need to answer it.

'You are my official mistress. Recognised.' He began, fumbling pompously over the words.

'Yes.'

'It would threaten the dignity of my position if you were to betray my trust.'

Silence. Astonishment?

'In such a case I would have to take steps to maintain my standing. Do you understand?'

'Yes.' But toneless.

'Do you see other men?'

'In this way?'

'In this way.' He kept his voice firm.

'No.'

He looked at her eyes and saw nothing reflected there. He felt a pain in his heart which he continued to fight but knew would win.

'There is no one but you,' she said.

'I am determined to keep you. No one else will have you.'

She lowered her eyes demurely and he felt first foolish, then irritated that this woman, who was not even wholly a native of the Black Land, seemed to have such power over him. No! He had survived too long by never allowing his feelings to rule him to give in to them now. He could control them as he always had, and always would.

He left her, already planning how he would break her spirit. He had shown weakness. Now he would only show strength.

From her window, Mutnefert watched Rekhmire shambling across the courtyard of her house, his outline barely visible in the dim light cast by the oil-lamps there. Beyond, in the darkness, there was silence. She could hear only his feet scraping over the flagstones, and the tiny lapping sound of the River. By and by, there was just the sound of the water; and then, as the wind dropped, even the River seemed to sleep.

She bathed vigorously, changed into fresh clothes, and carefully reapplied her make-up, calling her first body-servant to position the orange and white cosmetic cone of perfume on her head. Then she settled down to wait for her other visitor.

'I don't know what they are doing.' Aset was worried. 'But above all, I don't know why they are doing it. How is Rekhmire reacting?'

'He hasn't made any move,' replied Huy. 'But perhaps that is significant in itself. He hasn't been to see her at all. It is as if he had broken with her entirely.'

'No more regular visits?'

'None.'

'Then what is he doing?'

'He works on the palace all the time. The new king is due here in fewer than twenty days.'

'At least Amotju is recovered,' said Aset, doubtfully.

'More than recovered. But he still won't talk to me?'

Aset said no with her head.

The news she had brought disturbed him. Instead of going to the Northern Capital himself, to accompany the new pharaoh south, Amotju had sent his wife as his deputy. The gifts he sent with her would more than excuse his absence, together with his recent severe illness, which was known throughout the city; but they hardly explained it. His behaviour since had been even less easy to understand.

'Taheb left three days ago. Amotju suggested that I go with her too but I said no. Taheb and I do not make good companions unless it is for an evening only and there are others present.' Aset had smiled briefly, but instantly became serious again as she continued. 'Since then my brother has allowed himself to be seen openly with Mutnefert twice. Openly. Despite the fact that she is a high priest's official mistress.'

'Is he declaring war?'

'What else does it look like?'

'I don't understand. He was terrified of Rekhmire. He thought the priest had power over demons.'

'Perhaps Mutnefert has greater power over him,' Aset said with bitterness.

Huy thought for a moment. 'Perhaps he imagines himself safe from Rekhmire for now. The priest will do nothing until after the pharaoh is installed here. That is the most important thing—the maintenance of the status quo. After that, Horemheb will resume actual control, and Rekhmire—'

'Will do as he likes?'

'Judiciously, yes. There are no demons, only men,' Huy added, seeing doubt in her eyes. 'And Rekhmire is a politician, not a madman.'

'Are you sure there are no demons?'

Huy was not, but he still could not see their work. Demons, the gods and the undead were not the slaves of men, and did not operate rationally. And yet, he reflected, what was rational about Amotju's behaviour? Wasn't he tempting providence? Or had he suddenly gained power over Rekhmire in the form of some kind of information he could use against the priest? If so, from where had he got his information? There could only be one source.

'But I can't see Rekhmire confiding in Mutnefert. He confides in no one,' said Aset.

'What about Amotju?'

Aset laughed drily. 'He probably tells her everything. You know what he's like, and he's worse when he's drunk. Which is more and more frequently.'

'Why doesn't Taheb stop him?'

'I'd like to know that too. It's certainly not so that she can mother him.'

'Have you tried?'

'He doesn't listen to me.'

Huy turned and looked out over the city. They were sitting in the upper room of his little house, and it had a slight height advantage over its neighbours, so that there was a view over the rooftops to the River and the Valley in the west, and to the yellow cliffs bordering the eastern horizon. He wondered how secure he was. There had been no more death threats, and perhaps he was justified in thinking that whoever had delivered them was now confident that they had scared him off. On the other hand, there was the question of earning a living, to do which he would be forced to break cover soon.

'The sooner the better,' laughed Aset when he voiced the thought to her. 'Then you'll be able to get rid of that beard. You look like a Hittite!'

The days passed quickly as the Southern Capital readied itself to receive its new ruler—the first to take residence since the death of Nebmare Amenophis III, eighteen years earlier. The Black Land had never, in two thousand years, known such turmoil, and people in the cities were troubled. On the land, nothing had changed, and many had not noticed the changes. Years in this country were like days in others. Held at the centre of the world by deserts to the west and east, seas to the north and east, and an unknown and limitless forest to the south, the Black Land still basked in the knowledge that for two millennia its power had been uncontested and unshaken. Even the disgrace of the reign of the mad king, Akhenaten, which had brought shame to the country and the loss of the northern empire, had not brought the threat of ruin to the heartlands. Now, there was a new edict. Horemheb, through the new king, had declared the speaking of Akhenaten's name unlawful. Everywhere, masons were busy cutting it from monuments.

In the midst of this, however, Huy had little opportunity to indulge the sadness which he might well have felt as the ideals which he had supported and believed in vanished. He had to focus his attention on surviving here and now, however much his innermost thoughts might have yearned for a new country, where he could imagine transplanting the seeds of the enlightened thinking of his old king. Instead, he concentrated his attention on Rekhmire, who continued his administration of the temple work with apparently total single-mindedness.

He saw less of Aset, missed her, and hoped that she missed him; though it was for her own safety that he insisted that their meetings were infrequent. But sometimes she arrived unexpectedly, and then he was glad.

'There is news,' she said. It was urgent. They had barely greeted each other. 'It is Mutnefert.'

Huy was immediately alert. 'Is she dead?'

'No, but she has been threatened.'

'It was unlikely that she could continue as she has without so being. How did you find out?'

'Amotju told me.'

'Amotju?'

'Yes. He seeks your help again.'

'But you haven't told him where I am?'

'No.' Since he had gone into hiding, Aset had been the only one to know of his whereabouts. 'He was simply regretting that he had angered you, now that he needs you to help Mutnefert. Of course he believes that you are still in the city—or rather, hopes that you are.'

'If he cared about Mutnefert's safety, why did he allow himself to be seen with her publicly?'

'Perhaps that is something you can ask her.'

'What do you mean?'

Aset opened a small linen bag at her waist and from it drew a stone scarab—a plain thing, roughly carved in limestone. She handed it to him and he drew in his breath as he took it, and read the simple inscription on it.

'This is the second that she has received. It was she who asked for your help.'

'There has been nothing else?'

'I don't know.'

'Where is she?'

'At her house. She wants to see you.'

Huy looked at Aset. She did not return his gaze, and he could not read her face.

Mutnefert received him in the same room as she had before. She was dressed in a plain white tunic that fell straight from the shoulders to the feet, but which was gathered at the waist with a plaited coloured leather cord, attached with a silver buckle. Huy noted that it was silver, not gold. Nothing vulgar for Mutnefert. She greeted him warmly, even in her visible distress neglecting none of the social niceties instilled in her, offering wine and food before any other topic was broached.

She was taller and more graceful than Aset, Huy noticed, but this time he was more aware of a certain distance—or, perhaps more accurately, absence in her manner. It was as if a part of her sat secure within the personality she showed to the world, keeping its own secret, its own counsel, even at a time like this.

There was no mistaking her agitation, however. Her body and her hands were restless, having none of the repose which she had conveyed at their previous meeting. She looked at him with frank appeal in her eyes.

'It is good of you to come,' she began.

'I am glad to. But I do not know if I can help.'

She flashed a look at him. 'If you cannot, no one can.'

Huy spread his hands. 'Do you have the other scarab?'

She went to a small chest in the corner of the room and produced it. It was more or less identical to the one Aset had shown him, and to the one he had found himself outside the door of his room on the night he'd discovered Ani's body. It told him nothing new.

'Have there been any more threats?'

'No. But I am very afraid. I am sure that I am being watched.'

'Where?'

'Everywhere. Here... Wherever I go.'

'Have you any idea who it might be? One of the house-servants?'

'I have very few, and they have all been with me for a long time. I do not think one of them could have been suborned.'

'Then who?'

She hesitated, though clearly on the point of answering. 'You can treat me with confidence,' said Huy. 'Anubis could not keep a secret better.'

'Do you believe in the gods?'

This question caught Huy. It was not one he had expected from Mutnefert, whom he knew to be intelligent, but took to be conventional. In her beliefs, at least.

'Surely we all do,' he replied, and was rewarded by a frankly disbelieving, but still warm, smile.

'I haven't answered your question,' she said.

'You can always say, "I don't know."'

She looked down, rolling the scarab from hand to hand. 'I am Rekhmire's official mistress. But you know I am also the lover of your friend Amotju.'

'You kept it secret, at least from the world in general, for so long. Why have you tempted providence now?'

She looked at him: 'Do not tell Amotju what I am about to tell you; I begged him to keep it still a secret, but he wanted to dare Rekhmire, to make him do something he'd regret, to bring him down. It was my fault. I told him that I wanted to leave the priest, to get away from him for good.'

'That surely is not reason enough?'

She lowered her head. Huy admired the delicate arch of her neck above the simple silver and turquoise collar she wore.

'When I first came here, I had a position. The town was strong, it was the capital of all the Black Land. Although I was partly foreign, that did not matter. The king's own parents-in-law came from my father's country too. I had married an Egyptian. My husband was high in the administration of Shemau. Then, well, you know: Neferkheprure Amenophis—Ahkenaten, I mean—moved the capital north, and this city started to crumble. My husband lost his power, and died soon after. He was not a politician. Only people like Amotju's father, who could move with the times, flourished. Rekhmire comforted me. He was an outcast, like me, but stronger. It was a long time before I realised that he expected to be repaid for his kindness, and then it was too late.'

'But you kept your independence of him?'

'Yes.'

'But you needed his protection to survive?'

The head sank lower. 'Yes.'

Huy said, 'No one is going to blame you for wanting to survive.'

'I would feel more gratitude towards him, but—' she faltered. 'The man is a beast. He is worse in his appetites than Set. Now that I no longer need his protection, I want to be rid of him,' she concluded, in a firmer voice.

'So that you went out openly with Amotju to challenge Rekhmire's pride. You hoped he would do something sudden, rash, something violent, perhaps, which would bring about his ruin.'

'Yes.' She looked at him defiantly now.

'What made you think that he would? You know him. You know that if he was a man to give in to his feelings, he would never have risen as high as he has.'

'He knew I wanted to leave him, but he did not know why, or for whom. The fear of losing me made him love me.'

Huy fell silent in the face of this. 'What did you expect him to do?'

'It was Amotju's idea.' She spoke in a more controlled voice, though its tone was sullen. 'After what he had already experienced at Rekhmire's hands, simply as a result of political rivalry, he expected to draw the fire for this. He had prepared for it.'

'But Rekhmire is powerful enough to make his attack through intermediaries. He would never allow a crime to be traceable to him.' Huy still could not understand what had, in any case, brought about Amotju's change of heart. Whatever had happened to him during the period of his disappearance, he had been terrified by it.

'Amotju has introduced a spy into Rekhmire's household as a body-servant.'

'You will need more than one witness to condemn Rekhmire.'

'The man also reports to Horemheb,' Huy breathed quietly.

'Amotju was appalled at his experience in the afterlife. If Rekhmire has the power to send him there to be tortured into acquiescence, then Amotju must choose: either to give in or to destroy his destroyer. Rekhmire may be able to command demons; but he is himself a man.'

He reflected on how effectively Mutnefert had been working on his friend. Such a line of thought was certainly beyond Amotju. He looked at the woman with new admiration, won-dering at the same time about the developments which would undoubtedly occur when Taheb returned. It was inconceivable that Taheb had not left servants behind who would report to her what was going on in her absence. Was Amotju thinking about the same thing, or had the initiative passed from his hands altogether?

'But where does the spy come from?' he asked.

'You expect to be well trusted,' she said.

'You have trusted me too much already, by telling me all this.'

'He was in my late husband's service.'

Huy stood up.

'Are you leaving?'

'There is nothing I can do for you,' said Huy, simply. He was feeling outclassed and out of his depth. He was also disappointed. Rent was due on his house and there was the question of food and drink.

'But there is! You must find out—please—who sent me these.' She held up the scarab.

'But you know.'

'And who is shadowing me?'

'But you know.'

'But it must be confirmed. And stopped. And we have so few friends.'

'Your man in place with Rekhmire is in a better position—'

'But he cannot manage alone. He will help you. I'm frightened; and I know that Amotju trusts you more than anyone.'

She came close to him and he smelt the delicious odour of her perfume. Out of the corner of his eye he discerned a slight movement in another part of the room. The little red-faced monkey had appeared, and was scrambling to its favourite spot among the heap of cushions on the couch.

As he came away from the house, Huy wondered about the extent of Mutnefert's fear. He had not asked if Amotju would see him, but decided to risk calling on his friend. He crossed the city at dusk, assuming that Amotju would have returned to his house from inspecting his barges at that time, and in the hope of intercepting him before any intended visit to Mutnefert. He wanted to ask if the investigation into the death of Ani, from which he had been excluded, had borne any fruit, and he wanted to assess his friend's state of mind for himself. Before he had left her, Mutnefert had told Huy that she knew Amotju would be pleased to see him again, and that only pride stood in the way of his making the first move. Huy himself had long since dispensed with pride, but bringing the news of his acceptance of Mutnefert's request for help gave him the excuse he needed.

Shortly before reaching the house, he turned the corner of an empty street and found himself suddenly, inexplicably falling, in complete silence and utter darkness. The shock had been too great for him to feel anything but calm curiosity: who had dug this mighty pit, and why? And why, too, did he have the sensation of falling far more slowly than he would have in the ordinary course of nature, pulled towards the earth by the power of its own embrace? It seemed indeed as if some of the time he was not falling at all, but floating. He was still asking himself questions when the silence and the darkness swallowed him entirely.

The darkness and the silence continued, and so absolute were they that even when he became aware of them again his heart would not allow him to admit that he was...conscious.

Conscious. The word was a mockery of his condition. It was so dark that he could not see his limbs. He could not see the closest parts of him: his shoulder, his chest. He did not even know whether he was standing or lying. There was no sensation of ground beneath him; only the knowledge that he had stopped falling, or floating.

There were his eyes. He was aware that they were open. He could feel the tiny mechanism of his eyelids opening and shutting. When they were shut, his eyes felt protected. When they were open, they did not. There was no other difference. The darkness forced itself on to the surface of his eyes and if he had not felt so curiously relaxed he might have wanted to scream in panic at the suffocation of the light. He wondered how he could be so certain that his eyes were still capable of vision; how he, without more knowledge, could distinguish in his heart between the outer darkness he was in and the inner darkness which was blindness. His hand went towards the amulet he wore, the *udjat* Eye of Horus, sacrificed in the god's fight with Set, and redeemed for Man. Then his hand stopped. He wasn't sure if it was his hand, or something else moving.

Later, though he had no idea how much later, or even whether he had remained conscious all that time, he began to feel his arms and legs, his fingers and his toes, through the channels of his body. He found he could move them again, and extend them. He discovered that he could move his arms the extent of their reach. The legs were a more difficult matter. He bent the left one upwards, but found that he could not move his right. He lowered the leg again and repeated the experiment, bending his right leg. The effect was the same.

Now he felt his body with his hands. It was there. It had form. The passage of time was marked by the progress of his experience. He could even feel his kilt. His senses mocked him then by turning him around and over and over, so that he was swirling and tumbling like a leaf in the wind. The sensation was pleasant, and he gave in to it, though at the same time a part of his mind, far distant and barely acknowledged, was regretting that it had not been allowed time to complete the experiment—to reach down and try to touch whatever it was he had been standing on. If he had been standing. If he had been standing on anything. Then he came gently to rest. In another position. But what?

He held fast to one thought. He was in his body. He wondered if he should think about his past, and tried to, but then the effort seemed too great, despite the panic that seized him at the thought that he had forgotten. He did not even dare to say his name to himself, for *they* could hear unspoken words, and if *they* were listening, and learned his name, their power over him would be absolute.

So his heart spoke his name to itself, deep within its own fortress, where no one else could come: Huy.

He must be alive. Had he died, he would surely have come apart, into the Eight Elements. He revised his inventory of himself, more strictly this time, but still without haste, weaving through the velvet fog as through a maze to form the thoughts. He was aware of his *Khat*—his body; he must be using his *Khou* to be able to think at all. He knew his name, his *Ren*, because his heart, his *Ab*, had spoken it. But the other Elements, those that did not have a counterpart in life, he could not feel within him. Were they out there in the darkness? Was he dispersing into them? His *Ka*, his *Khaibit*, his *Ba*, his *Sahu*? He wondered if the dead had any memory of their lives. Surely he would remember the preparation for the tomb? Would his *Ka* not have appeared to take him by the hand and abolish the pain as they dried out his body with natron, burying it in the white sands? But even before that, would he not have remembered the plucking out of his corruptible parts, the brain, the physical heart, the bowels, the liver, the kidneys, the bladder, the intestines? Would he not have felt the pain caused by the embalmers' flint knives as they made the abdominal incisions, and then sensed the sweet agony of relief as they were drawn out of him by the long slender hooks, once decomposition had made them soft enough to be manipulated; taken out, the corruptible parts, to be dried in natron themselves and stored in the jars of the sons of Horus, to be replaced by packings of soft linen or clean resin to preserve his form? But what was this he was inhabiting now, if it was not the body he knew?

Who would have cared for him? Who would have paid the embalmers? He was alone. His own tomb was abandoned, half finished, back in the City of the Horizon. Already the sand would be blowing into it, already mice would have taken up residence there. Had anyone told Aahmes ? Who would bring food for his *Ka*? An ache of self-pity racked him.

Then he wondered if he could make sound.

He hardly dared to break the silence, and a new thought fought its way through the fog which softly clouded and clogged his heart: what if the sound should give him away? Was this a silence made to be broken? Or were there things in it as blinded by the dark as he was, but more used to it, able to sense and feel their way through it to him, guided by sound?

Summoning the courage to make a noise, something to keep him company if nothing else, he stumbled upon a new realisation: to make noise one must be able to breathe. A renewed wave of panic. Had he—even for a moment—been conscious of the act of breathing since his fall? Something else he hardly dared to confront; for if he was not breathing, he was dead. His heart was still caught in the soft nets of darkness, not unable to produce thoughts but fighting an overwhelming lassitude in order to do so. What did it matter if he were breathing or not?

But he opened his mouth and through what seemed many miles of filament a message came through to him, sitting in the centre of his body, that air was coming and going, coming and going. He decided to clear his throat.

He did so before he could start to think about the action more, and so allow fear to creep in and prevent him; but still no sound was produced, beyond a suppressed click as the air moved upwards into his mouth. Even so, that was enough to make him crouch, all senses alert. They could have heard that; even that. It had, after all, been a noise.

But then, if they were so sensitive, why should they not be able to smell him, if he still existed, as Huy, as a man? He was aware of his own smell, the smell of sweat now as he became fearful.

The softness again. The lassitude. Could it overcome even the urgency of fear? What position was he in? He was not uncomfortable, not cramped; but somehow he did not want to stretch out—afraid of what he might touch, if he did. He would wait. What else could he do?

But there was no time to wait. More sensations. In addition to the dark and the silence, now sensed and accepted as external impositions, there was temperature. Only now that he could sense cold—and from a certain direction, too—did he realise that he had been warm. What did the cold mean? His heart asked itself the questions and simultaneously wearily rejected them. Why did he torment himself with needless enquiries? Why didn't he just accept and give in? Sleep.

The next thing he became aware of, though after how long an interval he could not tell, for his heart was fogged and still would not operate to bring forth his thoughts all the time, was another smell, not connected with him. The air was still cold, and the coldness was still coming from somewhere, as far as he could determine, beyond the direction in which his feet were pointing. The smell was faint at first, and hard to identify, beyond that it was unpleasant. It came from the same direction as the cold. It was the smell of rotten fish and sulphur.

Huy gagged and rolled away, pushing at the ground with his feet, feeling rough stones on his back, until he struck his head on an uneven rough surface behind him.

Suddenly the darkness had dimension. He was somewhere. He was in a cave! But did that mean he was still in the world? His head swam as he struggled to regain some measure of comprehension, if not control, of what was happening to him; but reason kept slipping one step ahead of him. He had to be content with clinging to the impression that it was there somewhere. He felt liquid in his mouth, and immediately Time went into an elliptical course once more, and then not a course at all; Time itself, twirling and tumbling like a leaf in the wind. He was not aware of the darkness or the silence; they had fragmented, been invaded by blurs of colour and smudges of sound. Yellow, orange, brown, each colour flaring at the edges, each blending into the next and in turn taking up the whole universe; and mixing with them, blaring, like trumpets, but not trumpets, and fragments of speech that made sense while you listened, and none when you tried to remember immediately afterwards. Had he lost that ability? Comprehension is immediate remembering.

But then he did remember; and he trembled at what he knew must be before him. The crossing of the twelve halls of darkness to the Final Judgement. The Weighing of the Heart. But Thoth was lenient. No heart was thrown to Ammit, for the beast to devour. The forty-two judges never condemned. 'Oh my heart, rise not up against me,' he whispered, and felt for the scarab which the embalmers should have placed over his heart, to keep it from betraying his sins, folded into the bandages that wrapped him.

It was not there. His head felt light with panic as he scrabbled for it among the bandages. Where had they come from, he thought confusedly, as an age ago he had not been able to remember the process of his death. But now, he was wrapped as a mummy, he could feel the bandages; they were the one reality in this howling madness, where forces he could not identify were pulling, pushing, hurling him as the colours flared and the brutal cacophony of sound climbed to a scream that would not stop. Something was tearing at a part of him, at his hands, with rough claws and hundreds of talons—or were they teeth? Something was forcing his hands into the wetness of a mouth, and the teeth were closing round his wrists.

Jerking back instinctively, violently, twisting his body away in a horror that overcame every other sensation, Huy fell heavily, feeling as he did so another kind of pain, sharp but recognisable. Something was cutting into his chest; but it also cut through his confused consciousness. Shaking his head, he heard more sounds—but these, too, were familiar, and he struggled to recognise them. Voices. He could still distinguish none of their sense, but he was sure that they were voices. He opened his eyes. Instead of the darkness, a grey light swam into them. He couldn't focus. Once more he became aware of his body. No part of it was touching the ground. But he wasn't floating. He was being carried. They had lifted him off the ground and were carrying him somewhere. The grey light grew brighter, yellower, but still it was not bright. Evening then? Or dawn? Such times of day became possibilities again.

He knew that his chest was bleeding, and he knew why. He had fallen on the edge of his bronze amulet, his *udjat* eye. He could feel the slight pressure of its chain round his neck. As his heart clawed its way back to thought, he smiled inwardly. He would be as sick as a dog when he came round, when the drug had worn off; but his *udjat* eye had done its job; it had protected him, woken him up in time to realise what was happening to him. He lay as limply as he could. If they realised that he had come round, they would kill him. But where were they taking him now? Would they abandon him on the edge of the River, as they had with Amotju? Or had they other plans?

Aset was worried. For the third time in as many days she had knocked on the door of Huy's house in vain, and now Mutnefert had once again crossed the gulf of coolness that existed between them to ask her if she had any news of him. At first Aset had bridled when the approach was made, thinking that the secret of their love affair must be out; but after only a few minutes' conversation, in which she was able to plant two or three pointed questions, it became clear that Mutnefert had no idea that there was anything between Aset and Huy. It was simply that Amotju had heard nothing, and had suggested Aset as another possible source of information.

Aset told her brother's mistress that she had no idea of Huy's whereabouts, affecting a lack of concern; but added that she supposed he had had to go underground to find whoever had sent Mutnefert the death threats. Mutnefert had gone away, apparently satisfied with this explanation, but she asked that Huy get in touch with her urgently, as soon as he resurfaced. Aset agreed to pass on the message, but was careful to say that it was just as likely that Huy would contact Mutnefert directly.

'It's very important,' Mutnefert had insisted. 'I feel guilty that I may have endangered his life in sending him on a wild-goose chase.'

'What do you mean?'

She hesitated before replying: 'You know how things are, and I am aware that you do not like me because of it. We have never had a conversation about it because we have never...become close.'

'The possibility was unlikely to arise.'

'But I cannot explain to you without telling you something about the position I am in.'

'I have heard something of it. What do you mean by a wild-goose chase?'

'I have been trying to break with Rekhmire. He does not wish me to. As I—and Huy—already expected, the scarabs came from Rekhmire. He has now confessed it. It was an attempt to scare me, to make me throw myself on his mercy. So the mystery is solved.'

'Why did he tell you?'

'I don't know. Perhaps he saw that his plan was not working—that it was more likely to drive me away than bring me back.'

'What did you tell him?'

'That he couldn't force me to continue to be his lover.' Mutnefert lowered her voice to a whisper, ashamed of the predicament she was describing.

'What will you do when Taheb returns?'

Mutnefert replied evenly: 'That depends on Amotju.'

Aset knocked at the house door again, but she knew from the hollow sound within that there would be no reply. The house felt dead. She furtively glanced around in the street. Huy had chosen his lodging well; in this district of floating population, no one paid much attention to anyone else. She had dressed down to come here, and come alone, but she could not completely disguise her status, and the city was not so large as to provide perfect camouflage for her indefinitely. She wondered whether she was not worrying too soon after all; Huy had not set a limit on how long his investigation would take, nor had he described what he would do. But she felt responsible for him—no one else, even Amotju, seemed bothered by his disappearance, and Mutnefert was only concerned because of her involvement as his client. Since Huy had come into Aset's life, it had taken on a more exciting meaning. Her only regret was that he wasn't better placed to be a serious suitor.

The door was locked, but Huy had shown her the trick of it, and, with a final glance round, she reached into the hollow where the stone bolt was, and withdrew it.

There was little or nothing inside to tell her where he might be. The last person to see him had been Mutnefert, who had assumed that when he left her he had returned home—wherever that was, for she did not know. He had not mentioned any other intention, to her, and it had been late when they parted. It seemed unlikely that he would have gone either to Rekhmire's house or office in the palace that same evening. The lower room here had plain whitewashed walls, somewhat scuffed. Hanging from a hook by the door was a cloak, and a low table carried two or three unused rolls of papyrus and Huy's scribe's palette, on which had fallen a thin layer of dust. Two chairs were drawn up neatly side by side. Upstairs, the room contained a bed and another table. In an alcove, four clean squares of linen lay folded, and below it on the floor was a pair of very worn plaited palm sandals.

After the gloom of the house, the sunshine in the street made her squint, but she grew used to the light quickly enough to see a man who had been standing at the corner of the building opposite quickly disappear around it. Something about the speed of his movement told her that it was not a coincidence, and she followed him. He was a tall man and, despite the throng, it was easy to keep him in sight, while she herself hung far enough back not to arouse his suspicions, though this seemed to be an unnecessary precaution, because he plunged hastily on, never once looking back, and it struck her that he might be as amateurish as she was at this business.

As if to prove her wrong, at the next turning she was held up by an ox-cart, heavily laden with fish, lumbering across a little square where four roads met. She smelt the odour of fish on the men tending the cart, as they drove it on towards the salting sheds. Once it had passed, her quarry was nowhere to be seen. Her sense of disappointment was greater than she had suspected, but rather than give up, she followed her instinct and pushed on down the road which led towards the River. Jostled by the crowd, which increased in density as she approached the quay, she was rewarded by glimpsing the man again, the top of his head bobbing above the sea of people fifty paces ahead of her.

Earning one or two curses, she elbowed her way into the centre of the street, where she could move more quickly and freely, having only the carts and the occasional rickshaw to dodge around, and managed to keep the man in sight until they reached the waterfront. Once there, he turned left and made straight along the dock, past the barges loading and unloading, to where the ferries tied up.

There was even more activity here, and Aset was afraid that she would not be able to board the same ferry as the man she was pursuing, or, if she did, that he could not fail to notice her. She wondered fleetingly if he had recognised her, or if he had merely ducked out of sight and run at the sight of anyone emerging from Huy's house. She had not been aware of being followed on her way there, and over the time they had been together Huy had taught her to be cautious.

There were queues of jostling, gesticulating people, waiting in untidy lines for a confusing number of ferries. Aset was used to having her own private transport, and didn't know which destinations these various boats were bound for: the west bank, or further up or downriver. Although the ferrymen were evidently calling out their routes, their voices were drowned in the hubbub of the crowd, and she was nervous of asking anyone. These people, whom she enjoyed mingling with, thinking it adventurous when she was with Huy, were frightening when it came to the question of talking with them. They smelt of sweat, of fish, of stale oil, of sulphur, and of the River. Their clothes were mud-coloured and dirty. Beyond them, the little black ferry-boats, with their precariously furled triangular sails, bucked dizzily on the flooding water—safe, she knew, and contained by walls built in her great-great-grandfather's time higher than the highest known level of inundation; but nevertheless daunting in its power, like a giant muscle.

The tall man had manoeuvred his way to the front of a queue. He was separated from her by about fifteen people, but he might as well have been on the other side of the River already.

'Excuse me,' said Aset to her nearest neighbours, trying to coarsen her voice. 'Can I get through?'

'What for?' a surly fat woman in front of her asked, pushing her back.

'It's my brother—I've got separated from him,' Aset improvised desperately.

'Where is he?' More suspicion.

'Over there.'

'Go on, let the poor little bitch through. She's not even queuing for our boat,' said a small, bald man with a hooked nose and an enormous, shiny belly. He used it to nudge one or two people aside and Aset slid gratefully past, in time to jump into the ferry just as the boatman was casting off. One or two people still on the quay hurled abuse at her, but she could not make out what they were saying and ignored it, keeping her head down. When she did look up, the tall man, at the other end of the boat, was staring ahead, in the direction they were travelling. The ferry heeled over slightly as the sail was raised, then settled and moved forward and across the water at a surprising speed. Aset felt the pressure of her neighbours' bodies all around her; someone's elbow dug into the small of her back, and her own face was pressed close to another woman's; their eyes kept meeting and flicking away.

The man got off at the first jetty, and Aset clambered after him, almost forgetting to hand over the small copper piece demanded by the boatman, a wall-eyed man whose breath was so vile that she gagged as he thrust his face into hers to ask for his pay. His stumpy teeth were covered with a white slime.

It was getting towards the sixth hour of day, and there were fewer people about now, as the time approached for the main meal and the afternoon rest. It was harder to remain inconspicuous, and Aset compensated for this by keeping further back. She seemed to have aroused no suspicion, for the man kept pressing forward, looking neither right nor left. Concentrating on him, she was unaware of her surroundings, beyond acknowledging to herself that she was in an unfamiliar part of the city.

Suddenly the buildings ceased to hedge around them, and she found herself on a narrow sandy plain, the town behind her, the River on her right, and the cliffs which bordered the eastern desert away to her left. About five hundred paces to the south one of the long walls of the palace ran, magnificently painted with hunting scenes. A strong young pharaoh alone in a light chariot drawn by two slim horses stormed after antelope and lions; in another scene, he stood over a writhing leopard, an arrow in its eye. In another, he brought down ducks and geese with a fowling-stick; and in yet another, from a high-prowed papyrus canoe, he speared wallowing river-horses and crocodiles. The colours were bright, and so fresh as to appear garish in the sunlight.

In the exact centre of the wall a high dark entrance gate was built, its lintel and supports of heavy grey stone blocks. The tall man was making towards this. There was nothing else for it but to follow, and Aset did so quickly, needing to reach the gate in time to see which direction he would take once he'd passed it.

The palace was not one building, but a second city, encircled by walls. From where she stood by the gate she saw the man enter a low, rust-coloured edifice whose entrance was flanked by heavy columns with lotus-capitals, near which lay giant statues of Amun's animal, the ram. Here, the streets were more populous again. People hurried about their business in great preoccupation, for the time before the king's arrival could now be measured in days. No one paid attention to Aset, especially as she was quick to ape the same manner of harassed activity affected by everyone else. She dived into the building after her quarry, looking for some plaque or sign to indicate what the function of the place might be. Doors opened off the central corridor into unadorned rooms in which she could glimpse men bent over plans. Several of them wore the regalia of senior priest-administrators.

The tall man finally paused at a door which he opened without knocking on, and immediately closed behind him. Frustrated for a moment, Aset noticed a stairway built into the wall by the door which she guessed must lead to a gallery leading on to the room he'd entered. She ran up it and found that she had been right. Two painters were working on inscriptions and scenes which were to form a frieze round the gallery, but beyond a glance they paid her no attention. She looked over the parapet to the room below and saw that the man stood facing another across a broad table spread with papyri. The second man was heavy, and powerfully built, with huge, bunched shoulders. Even without the chain of office of the High Priest of Osiris he would have been unmistakable.

It had been a bad day's fishing for Anpu. The sun beat down on his back and the sweat ran into his eyes as he guided his little papyrus boat through the shallows along the eastern bank of the River north of the Southern Capital. The water level had risen to such an extent that the reeds which grew here only showed their tips above it, and it was easy to steer among them; but it was impossible to see fish because of the amount of red silt in the water, and the leather net came up time and again with nothing but weed clinging to it.

He screwed up his eyes and looked at the position of the sun, reckoning it to be about the tenth hour of day. The heat had lost its ferocity, but by this time in the late afternoon it had set its dead hand heavily on everything. The banks shimmered through the haze, and the oxen and the egrets seemed to doze even as they paddled at the edge of the water. Anpu decided to make for home. He would make an extra-early start tomorrow and try to make up his losses then.

He made his way to the stern of his boat, picked up the paddle and drove it lazily into the water. The light prow swung round instantly and he angled it into the stream of the current, pushing down hard to overcome the inertia. Looking up after the fifth stroke to make sure he was still holding the boat's bow directly upstream, he saw the body, resting against the capsized trunk of a palm. Quickly he made his way over to it, throwing a rope over the tree to secure the boat.

The current was strong, but as the River was so wide, its thrust near the bank was sluggish, so that although the boat was light, it was a relatively simple matter to bring it parallel with the palm trunk and lodge it there. Getting the body aboard would be more complicated, and Anpu wanted to make sure that it would be worth it, though even if the man were already dead, no doubt there would be relatives willing to pay a good price for the retrieval of the corpse for burial. As he came close, however, Anpu heard a faint groan.

Bracing himself, and spreading his feet so that his weight balanced the boat, he leant forward and took the man under the arms, half lifting and half hauling him aboard. He fell on his face among the dozen or so grey mullet in the well of the little craft. Anpu managed to turn him on to his back and make him more or less comfortable before clambering past him to take up his position at the stern, where he had to dig in much harder with the paddle than before to get the boat going upriver again.

By the time they were within sight of the city, Huy was able to sit up, groggily, and take stock of his surroundings. At the same time, he had to fend off a number of questions from Anpu, who clearly regarded him with a mixed sense of ownership and suspicion. But in return he was able to find out approximately where the fisherman had found him, and so calculate how far downstream the current had taken him after he had been thrown into the water. Never had Huy been more grateful for his powerful, stocky, unscribe-like body as he strove to swim to safety under the cover of darkness. He had wondered whether or not the intention of his captors had been that he should die; it seemed unlikely after having gone to the trouble of drugging him and subjecting him to a piece of theatre which had been sufficient to scare Amotju, and was certainly intended to have the same effect on him. But perhaps, being less important than Amotju, he had not been the subject of such precise orders as had been given for his friend's treatment.

They hadn't robbed him, in any event. His leather purse was still attached to the girdle of his kilt, and it still contained the couple of *debens* of copper he had had with him at Mutnefert's. These he gave to Anpu; the first as a reward, the second to buy his silence and to persuade him to let him off the boat before he reached the main quay. Feeling that he hadn't done so badly from his day's fishing after all, Anpu left his charge several hundred paces north of the city, pushed off, and made his way back to his village, already framing in his mind the tale of the rescue which he would tell to his fellow villagers.

Huy was certain that his captors had remained convinced that he was unconscious until the time that they dumped him—if they hadn't been, he was sure they would have killed him.

As it was, as far as they were concerned, their pantomime of the halls of hell had been successful. If it had not been for the real pain of his amulet piercing his chest, they might have succeeded as well as they had with Amotju, for Huy, despite his education in the court of Akhenaten, would not have doubted or questioned the evidence of his senses when the beginning of life after death, as it had been described in *The Book of the Dead* since the time of the ancient kings, was presented to him.

Walking cleared his head, and by breathing deeply and evenly he was able to rid himself of the nausea which plagued him. Gradually, his step became firmer, and he was able to begin to organise his thoughts. He began by taking stock of himself. There seemed to be very little physical damage, though his body ached and here and there large bruises were beginning to appear. Though he could not see what his face looked like, there was evidently nothing in his appearance to draw attention to him, as no one in the suburbs and then in the city centre gave him a second glance as he walked home. The decision to go back to his little house had been made easily: since he had been flushed out, there was little point in hiding now; and perhaps whoever had planned his entertainment would be less suspicious if he simply pretended that its designed effect had been successful. The plans he was now formulating would require secrecy of a different kind.

Arriving in the street in which his house stood, he paused for a moment to draw breath, for he suddenly felt tiredness descend on him. Looking up, he saw a light in the window of his upstairs room—it was so faint that he wondered if he had imagined it, but as he waited and the short dusk deepened into full darkness, the glow became more pronounced. Huy debated whether to go on, to find somewhere else, perhaps even to make his way to Amotju's house; but he found that his exhaustion would not let him. Whoever this was, they would have to be faced at some point. He made no attempt even to be stealthy as he opened his door, surprised to find it locked.

Downstairs, all was as he had left it. He shut the door behind him and went to the alcove containing a bundle of papyrus books behind which his broad-bladed bronze knife was casually hidden. It was still there, in an oiled leather sheath. He drew it doubtfully, aware that he was untrained in how to use it professionally, and crossed the room to the stone steps that climbed the opposite wall to the room above. He could see the light clearly through the square hole in the ceiling to which the stairs led. For an instant he stood still, listening hard, but no sound came from the room above. Then, slowly, he began to climb upwards. When he was nearly at the top, his head almost level with the opening, he paused again, and now he could hear a faint, regular, gentle sound—breathing. Gingerly, he raised his head so that he could see into the upper room. On the bed lay Aset, fully dressed. She had thrown a rug over herself and had fallen asleep.

She awoke with a start and looked at him in alarm; then he realised that he had not put the knife down. As she became fully conscious, she put her arms up to him and silently drew him to her. He closed his eyes and wished he could drown in her warmth.

Finally they drew apart. She looked at him properly now.

'What has happened to you?' she said in dismay.

'I don't know.' He wondered how he would begin to tell her. He glanced at Aset's face. To his relief it expressed more concern at his appearance than curiosity. If he had been less weary, he might have wondered why.

'How do I look?' he said, trying to joke.

She smiled. 'Terrible. I must clean your wounds.' There was nothing he wanted to do more than sleep, but after she had made him comfortable, she disappeared downstairs, to return with an earthenware bowl of water. With linen swabs, she bathed his face and hands, and he noticed for the first time that his knuckles were chafed and badly cut. There were minute pieces of grit in the wounds, and as he washed his hands, he noticed that under his fingernails there were quantities of fine red sand.

She held up a bronze mirror for him to see his face, which looked haggard and battered, but was still recognisably his own.

'I am going to try to cook something,' she announced. 'I have no idea how to, I have not been taught; but I have watched the cooks at home and I think I can manage. Do you think you can light the fire? Before I came I bought a duck and some fruit and *shemshemet*...'

Huy, despite himself, grinned, and realised that he was as hungry as he was tired. He made a fire in the oven, and produced wine and water from storage jars as she busied herself with splitting and flattening the duck, putting a copper pot on to boil white beans, and chopping onions and cucumber. Neither of them was good at preparing a meal, but there was respite and amusement in this unexpected, improvised domesticity which they both found comforting. As they worked, Aset told him about Rekhmire's spy.

'Did you hear what they said?'

'No. The two painters on the gallery began to take too close an interest in me; I had to pretend I'd taken a wrong turning, and go. But isn't it enough that Rekhmire sent someone to watch the house?'

Huy smiled. 'Yes.' He didn't add that he wasn't surprised. He knew more now than he would have imagined possible even a week earlier, but still he had not formed a picture he was confident of showing to anyone else.

After the tension of her adventure, Aset was brimming over with remembered excitement.

'What made you come back here?' asked Huy.

'I didn't know where to look for you. I thought that this would be the first place you would come back to. I was going to wait one whole day and night, then leave you a message.'

'That would have been risky.'

'I wasn't thinking about safety. I was worried about you.' As they ate, Huy told her, as far as he could, what had happened to him.

'And the same thing happened to my brother?'

'Yes.'

'Do you know who did it?'

'They wanted to frighten him; they wanted to frighten me.'

'To scare you off?'

'Certainly.'

'Then they must be working for Rekhmire.'

'It's possible.'

She stared at him. 'Who else could it be? Amotju has no enemies here.'

'It certainly seems unlikely that anyone else would gain from this...'

She was silent for a moment, thinking. 'But are you sure it was what you say? That it wasn't a real experience? Perhaps the gods have their reasons...'

Huy held up his hands. 'These are real wounds—I must have been dragged across rough or stony ground, and the same must have happened to Amotju. And the red dust that was under my nails doesn't come from the Fields of Aarru, though I know where I have seen it in this world.'

'Where?'

'In the tombs in the Valley, on the west bank.'

'Then it must be Rekhmire. He thought that you were getting too close to uncovering him.'

'We have discovered nothing to connect him with the grave robberies.'

'He is a clever man.'

Huy had never lost sight of the grave robberies. Since the rifling of Ramose's tomb, there had been no more activity that he had heard of; but the time that had elapsed between his encounter with Set and now was short. It might be that Rekhmire, aware of their interference, had decided to deal with Huy and Amotju before continuing with his activities. But in that case, why had he not simply had them killed?

'He is trying to destroy my brother.'

Huy looked at her. It was possible, of course; but if that were so, there were more effective ways at Rekhmire's disposal than robbing Amotju's father's tomb and raiding one gold bullion barge. His thoughts turned back to the Valley. Many tombs were constantly under excavation there, as the great nobles and the rich men of the city would start building their homes for the afterlife as soon as they could afford to start them in this one. There was a whole community of tomb workers, master craftsmen, masons and ordinary quarrymen, established in the Valley. There were also private tomb guards.

'Do you know where Rekhmire's tomb is being built?'

Aset thought for a moment. 'There are two. He started one many years ago; now that his power has increased, he has begun work on a new, larger site nearer the centre of the Valley. But there are several guards posted there.'

'What about the old tomb?'

'I don't know. I don't know what plans Rekhmire has for it. Perhaps it is simply abandoned.'

'But if it were guarded?'

'To get past well-paid guards is impossible. If you could not buy their complicity, you would have to have as much influence with them as their employer.'

Suddenly, Huy's mind could manage no more. The wave of exhaustion which he had been holding back would be restrained no longer, and crashed over him in a flood. His eyelids drooped, and he thought that he didn't care about any of them—about Horemheb's empire-building through the young pharaoh, the imminence of whose arrival had set the city buzzing; about the shabby morality of Rekhmire and Mutnefert, Taheb's waspishness or Amotju's gullibility. They all wanted to bring each other down just to advance themselves. This was how the world was, and how it had always been; the ideals of the City of the Horizon had been a dream. They hadn't even been supported. People had gone along with them simply because their proponent happened to be pharaoh. If Akhenaten hadn't had absolute power, his theories would never have been written down, still less followed; as it was, they had blown away at his death like chaff in the wind. But he, Huy, was still alive in the world, and had to live in it and through it, somehow.

He felt Aset's cool hand on his forehead, and was grateful. There was a debt of friendship to her brother to discharge, and before he slept his orderly heart was already admitting to itself that it could not simply leave things as they stood. But once this was over, he would apply to become a scribe again; he would accept that life had changed, and avoid confrontation with it.

Until then, he needed to rest, for there was much to do.

CHAPTER 10

Offering him wine, Amotju welcomed his friend as if he had returned from a long journey—which, Huy thought, he had, in a way, though he decided to say nothing about his experience. Instead, he told Amotju about his talk with Mutnefert, and lied about how he had spent his time since.

'Have you heard from Taheb?' asked Huy.

Amotju looked at him shiftily. 'Yes.'

'What is her news?'

'She has only sent two letters by courier. She asks after the children, tells me of the preparations there for the king's departure. There have been final receptions, a state banquet…'

'What will you do when she returns?'

Amotju stuck his jaw out a fraction. 'I will tell her that I am going to divorce her. There will be no difficulty. There is an agreed settlement.'

'And then?'

'Huy, you are an old friend, but—'

'Of course; I am sorry. It is none of my business.'

'In any case, you will find out soon enough. But you should know that the only obstacle to my happiness and my ambition is the high priest. What evidence have you against Rekhmire that I can use?'

Huy waited for a moment before replying. 'I do not think there is anything for you to use against Rekhmire. I do not know how he funds himself, but there is no reason to think that he is helped other than by the temple.'

'Then how is it funded?'

'You know as well as I do that when Akhenaten diverted all temple income to himself, and to the Aten, many of the goods were withheld from him. Look at how fast the old religion has regained lost ground. There is no mystery there.'

Amotju spread his hands in impatience. 'Then are you saying that he has nothing to do with the tomb robberies, and nothing to do with the piracy?'

'I am sure he has not. He may be guilty of other crimes, but not of those.'

'How do you know?'

'There is no positive proof; but he has had me in his power more than once, and it would have been the simplest matter to have me removed.' Huy mentioned that he knew a man had been set by Rekhmire to keep a watch on his house; but he did not mention that Aset had discovered him and followed him to the palace.

'Then how will I destroy him?'

Huy was astonished at the rage in his friend's voice. 'What for?'

'Someone has been waging war against me!'

'It is not Rekhmire, however much he may rejoice at your misfortune. You know you aren't the only prominent citizen to have his family grave plundered, or the only man with business on the River to be a victim of pirates. You want to cast Rekhmire as the villain because you need a rival removed. Time is running out, too. I believe you wanted this business concluded before Tutankhamun arrives. Now, he will be here within days. Worse, Rekhmire has succeeded in completing the palace—at least, the royal apartments. That will do him no harm in the new king's eyes.'

'Or Horemheb's. What is the difference?'

Huy said nothing for a moment. Then he asked: 'Why do you want this power?'

'Perhaps to prevent it falling into the hands of men like Rekhmire.'

Why do you think you are better than he is, thought Huy, but did not ask the question.

'Mutnefert told me that you have placed a man in Rekhmire's household.'

Amotju pursed his lips. 'She should not have told you, but yes, it is true.'

'Why now?'

Amotju looked at him directly: 'I was afraid you could not finish the job.'

'You ordered me to leave the priest alone. Or have you forgotten your experience in the other world?'

'I have talked with friends since.'

'With which friends?'

'With Mutnefert.'

'Did she persuade you to place the spy?'

'Yes.'

'And what did she say about Rekhmire's demons?'

Amotju lowered his head. 'That if they were demons, and obedient to him, then I would remove the danger by removing him.'

'Wouldn't you fear the anger of his spirit?'

'Once in the spirit world, his earthly ambitions would be gone. I would only have to go to his tomb, and propitiate his *Ka* with gifts.'

Huy ran a hand briefly across his forehead. How quickly people accommodated their beliefs to their convenience.

'What has your spy had to report?'

'I do not think—'

'I am supposed to be working for Mutnefert. Do you want me to help her or not?'

'He has nothing to report; but he has only been in place a matter of days, and whatever else he may have to do, it is clear that for the moment, at least, Rekhmire will be fully involved in the final preparations for the pharaoh's arrival. Although yesterday Rekhmire announced that he was crossing to the Valley.'

'Why?'

'My man didn't say: I think it must be to inspect his tomb. My man was able to persuade him to take him along as his body-servant.'

'How did he manage that?'

Amotju smiled. 'Rekhmire's sexual tastes are wide. Amenmose is an attractive man and knows his job.'

Huy left soon after, refusing to stay for wine or the midday food. Despite the fact that the sun was now high in the sky, he made his way down to the quay where the ferries were moored, and managed to catch the last one before the afternoon rest to cross over to the opposite bank. Disembarking there, he hurried across the hot flagstones and past the small, low buildings which huddled around the dock. Ahead of him, like a curtain cutting off the narrow plain, reared the cliffs into which the tombs of the mighty were cut. Wrapping a linen scarf loosely around his head to protect it from the sun, he turned northwest and made his way towards the upper corner of the valley.

On his way, he passed the entrance to Rekhmire's new tomb. The imposing gateway consisted of a richly decorated lintel and supports, carved in relief into the rock face, which had been flattened and smoothed for some distance above and to either side of it. Outside, under an awning balanced precariously between four twisted wooden poles, a dozen artisans sat, lunching on flat brown loaves, sweet onions and beer. He walked up and greeted them. In his headscarf and worn kilt, he looked like one of them. He told them he was working on the refurbishment of the principal temple of Amun at Karnak, a building whose bulk could be seen easily from here, rising on the east bank. He refused an offer to join them in eating, but accepted a beaker of red beer and water, and squatted down to join them. He knew that they would be on their guard against any stranger merely arriving and asking precise questions about the layout and progress of the tomb they were working on, so he simply dropped a couple of discreet enquiries into the general flow of their chat, while parrying their queries about work on the temple. He knew enough about building from his days as a clerk at the City of the Horizon, during the frenetic period of its construction, to be able to give intelligent answers, and this allayed their suspicion. In return, he was able to discover that work on this tomb had only been in progress for two years.

'The high priest is forty years old. He expects to live for another thirty,' said the foreman, as one imparting important confidential information. 'So he wants the accent here to be on quality. He doesn't mind how long it takes.'

'Who will look after it when he dies?'

'What do you mean?'

'Well, he has no children, has he?

'He has time to beget some yet.'

'He'll be lucky,' said one of the artisans. The foreman turned on them, but no one met his eye.

'Have you begun to paint?' asked Huy, referring to the intricate decoration, depicting scenes from the high priest's life, as well as illustrations of the world to come, and things and people he would need for his life there, which would be placed on the inner walls of the tomb.

'No,' said the foreman. 'We haven't finished excavating the transverse hall for the chapel, or the corridor beyond, yet. Then there's the shaft to the burial chamber to be dug; but we'll do that when the artists are working on the decorations for the chapel.'

'Does Rekhmire visit often, to look at progress?'

'When he can; he's a busy man.'

'Especially now.'

'Yes!'

'So he hasn't been recently?'

'No.'

'Not yesterday or today?'

'No,' repeated the foreman, looking at Huy obliquely.

But by now, Huy had sufficiently gained their confidence to be allowed to look inside the tomb himself. It was blissfully cool and dark, and here and there shafts had been sunk from the rocky cliff above to allow light and ventilation to those working at the far end of the tomb, which already ran seventy paces deep into the rock. The floor was swept and smooth, and a glance or two told Huy all that he wanted to find out from his visit.

'I bet he has it well guarded,' he said to the proud foreman as they made their way back towards the sunlight.

'Oh yes. Mind you, someone's here most of the time, working. The first shift starts just after dawn, and then after the midday sleep we work on until just before the light fades.'

'We post twenty soldiers at the temple at night,' boasted Huy, hoping that his approximate guess would take the foreman in.

'Well, that's a state project,' replied the foreman, rising to the bait. 'But we have four men on; and the amount Rekhmire pays them, I don't reckon they'd be bribable, either.'

'So there wouldn't be much left over to pay for guards for his old tomb?'

The foreman considered. 'Shouldn't think so. Didn't he sell the site on?'

'No.'

'What's your interest, anyway?'

'He's a man whose star is rising.'

The foreman laughed, knowingly. There were plenty of people in the Southern Capital just now, running around seeking the patronage of those who had so recently been returned to favour.

The sun had passed its zenith by the time Huy hastened on, grateful for the relief that the cooling day brought. He passed gangs of workers returning to work, and the mid-afternoon silence of the Valley was now broken again by the muted but ubiquitous sound of hammers and chisels on rock, as armies of men laboured to excavate the final resting places of the elite. As he walked, Huy's thoughts turned once again, briefly, to his own neglected tomb. Where would he rest in the end, he wondered, now that his world had been turned on its head? If he were to die today, he would be put into one of the mass tombs, with a couple of earthenware jars of barley to keep him company in the afterlife, if he were lucky. He wondered why his countrymen clung to this belief in an afterlife, when within a generation their descendants forgot about them, ignoring the curses inscribed on the tomb gates which were to be visited on those who neglected to feed and care for the *Ka* of the deceased resting within.

But no doubts assailed Rekhmire. The high priest of the cult of the god of the underworld needed to assert both his belief and his status.

Huy was passing more modest tombs now—those belonging to officials of middle rank, and businessmen and women whose wealth did not permit them to excavate within the precise centre of the Valley. It was here that twenty years earlier, Rekhmire had begun his first tomb—even at the outset of his career, he was taking no chances with the afterlife.

The entrance of Rekhmire's original vault was set some way from any new building and it was considerably smaller than the new excavation his exalted position demanded, but Huy managed to find it without difficulty, and established that he was correct by deciphering the already wind-worn cartouche containing the priest's name at the side of the gate.

It seemed unlikely that anyone came here to stand guard. It looked as though no one at all had been here for several years. The entrance was partially blocked by rubble, which had either fallen, or was the result of dumping from other excavations. The rubble was overgrown with thistles and sparse, grey-green weeds, among which a large lizard darted, disturbed by Huy's approach. Huy climbed to the top of the pile and peered into the black hole which was all that remained of the entrance to the tomb; but it was too dark to see anything. Retracing his steps, he began to walk carefully around the great ship of a rock into which the tomb was carved, and which raised its humped back, overgrown with more weeds and thistle, out of the surrounding area.

He had reached its westernmost point and was about to start following its northern slope when he noticed the opening. It was no more than a slit, but it was a pace wide at its broadest point, and around it the ground was worn smooth and weed-free. By looking carefully, Huy could even discern a path which led directly up to it from the arid ground below, though some attempt had been made to scrape the undergrowth back over it. He checked his pouch for the firestriker and the oil-lamp he had brought with him, and, after a last look around, lowered himself through the hole and dropped inside the tomb.

It was lighter than he had expected, and as his eyes became accustomed to the gloom, he saw that this was because three or four of the ventilation shafts cut by the original workmen had not been filled, and they allowed pillars of sunlight through. He was standing in what must have been designed as the inner chamber, for at the far end were the beginnings of the digging work for the shaft which would have plunged vertically down to a small room in which the sarcophagus would have been placed. Directly above it, on a plinth, stood a statue. The pose was formal, but the head was startlingly lifelike, and although the body had been relieved of its bunched shoulders and club foot, the heavy face that leered down, though twenty years younger, was clearly Rekhmire's.

Underfoot, the ground was rough and uneven. Stooping, Huy could see that jagged stones protruded from the red sand. He felt one, and quickly withdrew his hand. It was a sharpened flint. Clearly at some stage, workmen had dumped their worn-out tools in this abandoned grave. But the stones had been disturbed. Grooves ran along the surface of the rough ground.

Someone had been dragged across it; but how recently?

He wondered when the work had been broken off. Five years ago? Ten? More likely earlier than later, for tomb-building here had come to a virtual standstill after the transfer of the court northwards. But even if no work had been done for a long time, there had been people here within the last days. There were the remains of two fires, and in one corner Huy discovered a handful of new copper nails.

Lighting the lamp, he moved carefully forwards through the linking corridor into the mortuary chapel, which would have originally led to a vestibule beyond which the outside world lay. Here, Rekhmire's *Ka* would have come to gather up the food offerings left for it. Although the tomb had never been in use, Huy shuddered involuntarily.

The chapel was much brighter, illuminated through the hole which represented the remains of the blocked-up entrance in the vestibule immediately beyond. The painters had started work here before the tomb was abandoned, for Huy saw that he was surrounded by rows of shadowy figures performing the day-to-day tasks which Rekhmire would expect to have done for him still when he reached the Fields of Aarru. He came across one scene which made him grow cold. It depicted Rekhmire on his journey through the twelve halls of darkness, encountering and quelling the demons that dwelt there, finally emerging into the Hall of the Two Truths, where he stood respectfully as Anubis weighed his heart against the Feather of Maat, and as Thoth-the-Ibis-Headed recorded the finding in the presence of the Forty-Two Judges. Beyond Thoth, the beast Ammit crouched, ready to devour the hearts of the unjust.

There were other things here, which did not belong to the tomb. A pile of discarded *shabti* figures—magic models of the servants who would care for a dead man in the next world. Huy picked one up and examined it; it was of river-horse ivory, overlaid in gold and set with carnelian, turquoise and lapis lazuli. Beyond the figures, all of which, Huy noted, were of the same high quality, lay a small quantity of loose gold nuggets. The gold was still in a pretty impure state, and the nuggets were of the kind formed at the mines in the far south, where the molten gold was dropped into water to form small, irregular lumps for ease of transport, when it was not desirable or possible to make ingots in rough moulds dug in the sand.

If the *shabti* figures were loot from a grave robbery, the gold was not. Huy knew where the gold had come from.

But there was more. Four broad leather slings hung from the wall, where a nail had been carelessly driven into the soft stone through a painting of Horus-the-Hawk-Headed. The leather was coarse and hard, and stained with dark patches where some liquid or other had soaked into it. The patches were new. Huy held one of the slings to his nose. There was the smell of leather and the smell of blood. Next to the slings hung something else. A crocodile mask of the same kind that had been fixed over the face of Ani when Huy had discovered his body.

Panicking at the memory this sight triggered, and at the realisation of where he was, Huy backed away, and hurried down the corridor towards the inner chamber, cursing himself for having left his line of retreat unsecured. In his haste, he stumbled, and fell on the floor, cutting his hands on the sharp flints. Scrambling to his feet, he reached up and hauled himself out through the slit into the blue twilight. His instinct then was to run in the direction of the jetties, but instead he made himself walk in as straight a line as was possible from the tomb towards the riverbank.

It was becoming too dark to see clearly, but there were recently overturned stones and the broken stems of plants to guide him. In any case, the shortest route would be the obvious one to take if you were in a hurry and carrying, or dragging, a heavy weight. Huy had no idea how fresh the blood was, but he knew that if he could still smell it above the heavy odour of the ox-leather slings it could not have been shed more than twenty-four hours earlier. Neither he nor Amotju had bled copiously, except from the hands when they had been dragged across the flint floor. The slings from which they would have been suspended to give them the impression of weightlessness when they were drugged would not have been stained with their blood.

He hurried on and arrived at the River's edge before the short dusk was over. Every day the water was rising, and now its colour was turning from green to red. But the level was not increasing as fast as expected. Huy came upon an area where several large flat rocks shelved down to the water. Here, despite the lateness of the hour, there was a hubbub of excited activity. Among a cloud of buzzing flies, seven or eight vultures hopped and flapped, shaking their naked red necks and then dipping and bobbing to feed again on what looked like an irregularly shaped small black hillock, half in and half out of the water. As he approached, the wind brought the stench to Huy's nostrils and his stomach churned, but he made himself press on. The large birds regarded him with irritation and suspicion, but they did not retreat. As he drew close, one dropped its head and came up again quickly, a long strip of red flesh dangling from its beak.

There were two bodies, thrown untidily together so that they were twisted round each other. Both faces were turned upwards, and Huy could see that the eyes had already gone—pecked away first so that the birds could probe through the holes they had made and fish with their naked heads for the brain beyond. One now had its head buried ostrich-like in one body. A second was poking and pecking its way towards meat through the anus of the other corpse.

One of the men had been killed by a sword thrust from behind. The other, more badly cut about, had put up a fight. Huy didn't recognise the body, though there was enough of the face left to make recognition still possible.

The first man was older and heavily built. Drawn in death, the face retained its stubborn strength, and in the gathering darkness the sightless hollows that had held his eyes still seemed to concentrate power. His hunched back raised his supine body slightly, so that the head had fallen back, and the club foot was twisted inwards. A vulture, staggering along at that end of the rock, lost its balance momentarily and to steady itself grasped the foot firmly with its claw.

There were fifteen barges, spread out across the entire breadth of the widening River, sailing upstream in delta formation. At the centre of the 'V' was the golden royal barge, its ornate prow thrusting through the red water, pushing it aside. The north wind blew steadily behind the boat, filling the golden-tasselled sail. The rowers had an easy time, but their shipmates on the consort barges had to strain to keep up.

The smaller barges which formed the escort were all merchantmen converted, for the purpose of this journey, into warships: their decks were cleared and each carried a contingent of marines equipped and financed by the boat's owner. The royal flagship, the king's own chief boat after the royal barge, sailed at the apex of the flotilla, and third from it on the eastern wing of the 'V' was *Splendour-of-Amun*. Taheb stood amidships on the starboard side, looking across to the royal barge, where she could see the boy-king seated under a white linen awning, cooled by peacock-feather fans wielded by massive Nubian body-servants. His skin was a light copper colour, and his body spindly and slightly stooped. His face bore a strong resemblance to Akhenaten's, though the eyes, even at this distance, were harder.

Taheb considered the years ahead which would bridge the gap between now and the young king's majority. Any battles for power, she concluded, would be won and lost in the first months, in the court—as she called it in her mind—of Horemheb. What the king would do to curb the general's powers when he attained his majority at thirteen, she had no idea. In a staggeringly short space of time, the general had not only dissociated himself completely from the old regime and the cult of Aten, but had collected a more impressive array of titles than had ever been bestowed upon any commoner in the history of the Black Land. Taheb knew to which star she needed to attach her chariot. Horemheb was now Greatest of the Great, Mightiest of the Mighty, Great Lord of the People, King's Messenger at the Head of his Army to the south and north, Chosen of the King, Presider Over the Two Lands and General of Generals.

It was a pity, she thought, that she had not been able to secure a place on the royal barge itself; but there was adequate compensation in the placing of *Splendour-of-Amun* in the flotilla. The barge held the highest position of any not owned by a noble, and this despite Amotju's absence. Her thoughts raged in frustration at her husband. How weak he was! But if she were to be able to pursue her own ambitions, she would need him for a time yet. Perhaps the scribe, Huy, would have good news for her at last; that would be some compensation, for her patience was running out, and she had hoped that the battle with Rekhmire would be over before the arrival of the king.

On the jetties and quays on either side of the River at the Southern Capital, great crowds glittered in clothing of white and gold. As soon as the ships came within view, music struck up, and despite the distance still to cover, the water carried to them the sounds of the instruments, dominated by the *chakachakachaka* of the sistra.

The king was standing now, and, clearly excited, ran forward to the prow of his barge, followed by two of his attendants carrying broad fans to shade him. They persuaded him to return to his seat, and busied themselves in placing the *pschent* upon his head—the red-and-white double crown of the unified Black Land.

It took another hour to dock, and it was an hour after that before Taheb thought it in order to withdraw. She had managed to catch the king's eye twice, and to exchange smiles: something which in theory was forbidden, but the king was young, and she was determined to impress her face on his memory if she could. Horemheb had been there, but at this public reception his stern face would give nothing away, and he refused to meet any eye but the king's, who for his part returned his gaze with an odd expression, partly of fear and partly in appraisal, as if he were looking at a strong horse which needed breaking—but which could throw him and kill him in the exercise.

She had looked around in vain for Amotju, or Huy; which irritated her, though a carriage had been sent from the house. She was pleased to see that it was the best they owned, and had been decked out in as rich a fabric as she could have wished. The servants who had accompanied it, she noticed, were not her own personal body-servants, from whom she would immediately have sought news of the household; but Amotju's driver and ox-groom.

At her house, she found Amotju waiting for her in the white limestone courtyard. Even within the short period of their absence from each other, his health had grown considerably better; and she noticed that although the day was relatively well advanced, there was no sign that he had been drinking.

He looked at her so sombrely that the rebuke on her lips for not meeting her at the quay died, and her ill temper was replaced by curiosity. They greeted each other formally, and she noticed an even greater restraint in his manner than she had been aware of formerly. Perhaps it would be simpler if they gave up all pretence that they still had feelings for each other, she reflected, balancing the pros and cons of the new situation coolly. As a divorcee her standing would be adversely affected; but then, so would his. She doubted, however, if his ambition was as strong as hers.

They stood regarding each other, neither of them anxious to be the first to speak. From the inner courtyard, Huy emerged. He, too, looked preoccupied, and though his eyes met hers for a brief instant, they quickly flicked away again. This was new, too, she thought. He had always been frank, at least; now he seemed to have become as shifty as any other Southern Capital intriguer.

'You look like conspirators,' she said, finally.

'Are you tired?' her husband asked in a strained voice, leaning against the back of a chair.

She looked at him in increased surprise. 'It has been a long enough journey, but hardly exhausting. Why didn't you come to meet me? You have missed a chance to be presented to the king. He was expecting you.'

'The king will have other matters to occupy him very soon. Even now, they are probably telling him whatever version they have dreamt up.'

'What are you talking about?'

'If you are not too tired,' Amotju said,—and could she be mistaken, but was he not speaking sarcastically?—'Huy will tell you what has occurred in your absence.'

He turned on his heel and disappeared into the house. She turned to Huy, fighting to preserve her dignity in the face of this monstrous insult in front of a stranger.

Huy had been looking at the ground; now he looked up, with an expression which might have been sympathy. How dare he presume to sympathise with her? He was lucky to be in their house at all—he should have been in exile. She bridled. She would speak to Horemheb. She would—

'Rekhmire is dead,' said Huy.

Every other thought fled from her heart. Her mouth was dry.

'I do not know how many questions you will have about this. I know that you will not be sorry. I found the bodies of Rekhmire and the spy whom Amotju had placed in his house by the shore on the west bank near the priest's abandoned tomb. They had been killed at the tomb and dragged to the water's edge...'

Taheb's mind was racing. What spy? What had Amotju been doing behind her back?

'Whoever left them there miscalculated the rise of the

flood, or they would have been swept away. As it was, the vultures got them. I raised workers from the nearest encampment and we dragged the bodies clear before the crocodiles arrived.'

'When—?'

'Two days ago. Your timing is good.'

'What do you mean?'

'To have returned now. You might have been suspected.'

'How dare you?'

Huy smiled. 'Don't worry. I knew how ambitious you were; but I was sure that you would draw the line at having Rekhmire killed. You must have been frightened after Ani's death, though.'

Taheb said nothing.

'I was certain that Ani would never have taken steps to incriminate Intef on his own initiative, despite his boasting, and his strong reasons for doing so. Intef was guilty of piracy no doubt, but there needed to be conclusive proof. Planting the case of gold was your idea. Ani took it from the unloaded cargo and you made sure it was not recorded.'

'What would you have done?' she said defiantly. 'We couldn't have our barges robbed and not retaliate. There had to be a punishment. You said yourself, the man was guilty.'

'And who do you think was behind the piracy?'

'Rekhmire, of course.'

'No.'

'Then who?'

'The person who had him killed; the same person who had Ani killed. You are next on the list, though it may be that she will wait until Amotju has divorced you. If you die before, it would do him harm; and she wishes your husband no harm. I think she loves him, or at least wants to possess him. In some people that is one and the same thing. It has been her undoing, but everyone has a weakness that will bring them down in the end. The depth of the fall depends on the height of the ambition.'

Taheb felt her scalp crawl. She had walked straight into a

nightmare. What was this squat little ex-scribe talking about—Amotju planning to divorce her? But she had to continue to listen.

'I am not telling you all this to hurt you; but you are my employer. You asked me to get to the bottom of this. If I had been trained for the job, I would have done so sooner; and lives might have been saved.'

'You had better tell me all you know, then. Wait,' she added, as another thought struck her. 'How much have you told Amotju?'

'Not quite everything.'

'He is angry with me.'

'Yes.'

'You mentioned divorce. Did you plant that poison in his heart?'

'No. Surely you knew he had been planning it for some time?'

'But no!' She was outraged that her husband had managed to deceive her so successfully; but the greater part of her mind was already working on how much of her ambition she could salvage from this mess.

'That is a domestic problem between you which certainly doesn't concern me. The killings do. Horemheb has called out every Medjay in the city to seek Rekhmire's murderers. It will not take him long to establish the identity of the man found with him, and trace him here.'

'You have said nothing.'

'I do not have Horemheb's ear. As far as he is concerned, I no longer exist in this city. After I had led the workmen to the bodies, I disappeared; it was they who reported the matter. But do not worry. We will have delivered up the killer before suspicion can fall on this house.'

Suddenly Taheb knew who it was. 'Mutnefert.'

Huy sighed. 'Mutnefert. That is something your husband does not yet know. I will need your help when I tell him, though

I do not know whether he will be convinced, or whether the knowledge will affect your lives together. He was divorcing you for her.'

Taheb turned her face away. She felt sick. She wondered whether she cared to hear any more, but she had to know. 'It isn't possible,' she said. 'No woman would be capable of such crimes.'

Huy smiled. 'Amotju is angry with you because he knows that you were in collusion with Ani to secure a prosecution of Intef. At first, of course, he was grateful; but as I told him more, his resentment grew. Intef was Mutnefert's brother. Half-brother, but they were very close. Their father came from Mitanni. He came to the City of the Horizon as part of an embassy to Akhenaten, and stayed. It wasn't difficult to check records, once I had realised that they had the same background in common, and even looked similar. Amotju loves Mutnefert, or thinks he does.'

'It is good of you to tell me.'

'I know these things wound, but you must know the truth to understand.'

'You do not think I care.'

'Let me continue. Mutnefert had established herself as the official mistress of Rekhmire before she met your husband. As her own security grew, so she needed Rekhmire less, and grew less tolerant of him. For his part, as he sensed her growing cooler, so his need for her grew. In the end the only way he felt he could keep her was by force. That meant discovering her secret. He knew that her wealth was created, not inherited, and he knew that from him she derived power and position more than material wealth; but it wasn't until Intef was arrested and executed that he made the connection between her and the piracy. The grave robbing he already suspected. He had a note passed to me anonymously which enabled me to go and witness the breaking open of Ramose's tomb. Obviously he had learnt early on that I was working for your husband and hoped that my investigation would lead to her, and send her running to him for protection; but he underestimated her. She had posted guards of her own at the perimeters of the tomb, and as she had a taste for the theatrical, she had dressed them as demons. One of them came across me, and surprised me. To add to the effect, which certainly terrified me at the time, he had been daubed with a paste of fish-glue and sulphur—the smell of the underworld, and which is used by shamans in Mitanni. Otherwise, he was just a large, strong man, with a bronze armshield, and wearing a crocodile mask. That ought to have been enough to scare anyone off.'

'Why didn't he kill you?'

'The only deaths that took place were ones Mutnefert thought necessary.'

'And yet she didn't draw the line at mocking the gods.'

'Yes. But she had no belief in them. She told me so herself, not in so many words, but through hints and actions. I think she felt so secure by that time, though, that she could not resist the urge to show off, to court danger—but then, she underestimated me.'

'What happened to Amotju?'

'He was getting too close to the truth, and he had engaged me to help him. She was afraid that the path he thought would lead to Rekhmire might lead him—and me—to her. She wanted to frighten him in such a way as to cast blame in the direction of Rekhmire. And as Rekhmire grew more desperate about losing her, so, she hoped, he would become incautious enough to bring about his own downfall. She wanted to be rid of him, but she wanted to draw the teeth of his power too.'

'But how?'

'The man from your household—Amenmose—whom Amotju sent as a spy to Rekhmire. She told me, and she may have told your husband, that he was also reporting to Horemheb; but that was untrue. He was working independently for her, as he had once been in the service of her own late husband. She felt safe enough to tell me that herself. By that time, Rekhmire was getting close to the truth about her operations, and knew, too, that she was having an affair with Amotju.

Mutnefert wanted Amotju to flush out his rival fast, before Rekhmire had gathered enough information to blackmail her into staying with him.' Huy smiled grimly. 'As soon as you had left for the Northern Capital, she persuaded Amotju to be seen openly with her, knowing that it would bring matters to a head, since Rekhmire would have to react.'

'How could she have known that I would agree to go?'

'Amotju had no secrets from her. He was her principal source of information. She knew about the gold shipment from him; she knew the extent of your ambition through him. She knew how to get at me, through him.

'But as the situation changed, she had to adapt her plans. At first, she tried to throw me off the scent by getting Rekhmire to persuade Horemheb that I was undesirable. Then there came the need to avenge her brother's death, in which she knew Ani was the main player. The nature of Ani's death was by way of a warning to me. The cruelty was not gratuitous. I was ready to heed it, but then I had a row with your husband which determined me to stay: the fight had in any case become personal. Amotju told Mutnefert that I had gone to ground somewhere in the city, and she, mistaking Rekhmire's investigation of her for mine, decided that she needed to find me, to give me one more warning that I couldn't ignore.'

'She could have killed you.'

'I know. I think it was more important to her to defeat me by fear. What had worked with Amotju would work with me. And—forgive me—Amotju was as soft as silt in her hands. When it suited her to convince him that his experience in the underworld had been engineered by Rekhmire in order to persuade him to challenge the priest directly by appearing in public with her, he was more than willing to believe. Wine helped, and you both encouraged his drinking, didn't you, for the same reason: to keep him malleable.'

Taheb said nothing.

'I was groping in the dark; I had not begun to suspect

Mutnefert, and I needed work. She approached me through Aset, who has no love for her, and even managed to convince her how much she needed my help. She spun me a story of nonexistent death threats, and of being shadowed—perhaps by agents of a jealous Rekhmire; and at the same time she tried to assess the extent of my belief in the gods. She expressed cynicism in them, which, as a half-Mitannite, she could perhaps have done; but I noticed how casually she handled the scarabs on which the death threats had been inscribed. I do not know if I convinced her that I believed, but in any case the die was cast. She had made me break cover, and already her plan was laid. I was to be subjected to the same passage through hell as Amotju.'

'What did she hope to achieve?'

'She hoped to warn me off, finally, or to convince me of Rekhmire's guilt. Either way, she would have been happy. In any case, events were not moving fast enough for her. The days left until the arrival of the new pharaoh were passing quickly: you would return, and with the installation of the king at the palace, Rekhmire would be in a position of almost unassailable power. She had to force the pace. She had to be free of Rekhmire, and the path of Amotju's political ambition as she saw it had to be cleared. She was sure he would divorce you; after that, in time, she would, I am certain, have had you killed. Everything would then be as she wanted it.'

'So she murdered Rekhmire.'

'Yes.'

Taheb looked around her quiet courtyard and it seemed to her that she had never seen it before in her life. The house was still, for the sun had passed its zenith, and the shadows on the wall were deepening. She wondered where in the house Amotju was, what he was doing, what he was thinking.

'Mutnefert had used Rekhmire's old tomb as the scene for the journeys beyond life. We were drugged, and then it was simply a question of guiding the hallucinations we had. But she used the place as a storeroom, too. It was ideal; abandoned, at some distance from any other excavations, and yet close to the River; and Rekhmire had not sold the site to anyone else.'

'How did she get him there?'

'I don't know. How would you have done it? Perhaps by pretending to give in—to show him her centre of operation, and so put herself completely in his power? He would have been flattered and relieved. Of course, she could not hope that he would come completely alone; but she had enough people to deal with Rekhmire and any bodyguard.'

'So—poor Amenmose.'

'Yes. He was doing his job. I suppose she felt she could not trust him. He must have put up quite a fight.'

'Would she have been there?' Taheb was intrigued by the details despite herself, and wondered if she would have been similarly capable.

'I think so; she would have wanted to see that the job was done properly.'

'What is she doing now?'

'Waiting for Amotju to tell her that he has spoken to you. Receiving the news of Rekhmire's death with horror.'

'What must we do?'

'You must decide. I think we must tell Amotju everything now.'

But Amotju was nowhere to be found.

Why would he do this, Taheb kept asking herself as they hurried through the town. Why? Next to her, Huy remained silent. He was cursing himself for his amateurishness, for his inability to account for human behaviour, for his stupidity in underestimating his friend, and the power of his friend's love.

They would know soon enough if his worst fears were justified. Hurrying on foot through the town, pushing past the late afternoon crowd, denser than usual on account of the celebrations due to the king's arrival, they were hot and tired; unlikely partners called upon to make one last effort when they had assumed none to be necessary.

Taheb stumbled over a badly set flagstone and Huy reached out to support her arm. He was surprised at how strong she was.

'Thank you.'

'Are you all right?'

'Let's just get on.'

They were held up for minutes as a procession of priests solemnly carrying wooden figures of Amun, together with his wife, Mut, and son, Khons, passed across their path to the music of sistra.

'Could you be mistaken?' asked Taheb, knowing that she was clutching at last hopes.

'If he isn't there,' Huy replied, 'I will be happy. But I cannot see where else he can have gone. I asked him to leave me alone with you to begin with, and to trust me. But of course he must have simply listened at a window. It would be the most natural thing in the world.'

'How much can he have heard before he left?'

'Enough to warn her. But if he had heard everything, I think his reaction would have been the same.'

Taheb was silent, hearing this, and Huy bit his lip. He had not wanted to hurt her by exposing the power of her husband's love for a murderess; but who could possibly have predicted anything of the sort, he told himself. Who could have foreseen anything so unreasonable?

Their shadows danced across street walls dyed a deep yellow by the sunshine of the eleventh hour of day. A litter toiled past, moving with infinite slowness through the throng, its irritable occupant leaning out to shout at passers-by.

'Will they still be there?'

'He had a fifteen-minute start. He'll have to explain to her. With luck they'll still be there.'

'What if she's killed him?' Taheb blurted out. Huy was silent.

'I cannot believe this is happening,' said Taheb, more quietly.

They hurried on in silence, climbing a steep street which reached its peak after thirty paces and then descended again just as sharply. Around the corner and across a small square stood Mutnefert's house. As they drew near, they unconsciously slackened their speed, trying to control their ragged breathing. Taheb felt curiously calm; Huy struggled to plan a strategy, and failed.

The door of the house stood ajar. Cautiously, Huy pushed it open. Beyond, the courtyard was silent. Entering the inner rooms, and passing through them, they found no one. There was no sign of struggle, or any hasty departure. Everything seemed to be in its place: there was not even the suggestion of an interrupted dinner. Only when they came to the room in which Mutnefert had received Huy did they become aware of movement behind the door. They opened it, and there was a frantic scampering. Then, from its place on top of the pile of cushions, the little red-faced monkey hissed and bared its teeth, glaring at them with furious, desperate eyes.

There was little activity at the quay, but Taheb managed to track down one of the harbour-masters who told her that he had seen two people set off downriver in a hunting boat only a short time ago. People frequently went after wading birds and duck in the early evening when they would be feeding; but on this particular day he had to admit that he'd thought it odd because nearly everybody was celebrating the arrival of Nebkheprure Tutankhamun.

'Can we follow them?' Huy asked Taheb.

'There's *Splendour-of-Amun*. But I don't know about the crew, or how long it'll take to get her turned round and ready.' She spoke automatically, as if in a dream.

'I know what you are going through,' said Huy.

'Do you?' she replied sharply. Her eyes were too bright.

Quickly, they made their way along the front to where *Splendour-of-Amun* was moored. They hurried aboard and Taheb raised the boatswain, who was drinking black beer with the three men who had been left on guard while the rest of the crew joined in the celebrations ashore.

'We can't sail her on our own,' said the boatswain, looking at Huy suspiciously after Taheb had made her request.

'We are going downstream,' said Taheb. 'You have enough men to steer her.'

'But not to get her back.'

'We don't have to worry about that.'

The boatswain looked doubtful. 'I don't know. Now that we're home, I'd need to ask the captain—or the owner.'

'I am the owner's wife.'

'I know, but—Look, it'll take half an hour to get her going. It will be dark. Why do you want to go now, anyway?' His gaze moved from her to Huy again.

'We'll take the skiff,' Huy said. 'We will take your three

men to crew it, and you stay with the barge. When we return, you will be reported to the owner.'

The boatswain gave him a dark look, but turned and shouted a curt order. The men got to their feet and made their way forward to where the skiff was cradled. They swung the little boat out and lowered her into the water. They had already drunk plenty, and misjudged the drop, so that the skiff crashed down nose first. But she righted herself, and the sailors climbed aboard, swiftly followed by Taheb and Huy.

Once out in the stream the cool wind and the steady, easy work of rowing with the current calmed them. The sun was setting blood red over the horizon beyond the Valley, and Huy could make out the lonely black mound of Rekhmire's old tomb against the glow, devoid of significance to anyone there but him, and he did not point it out to Taheb. She sat stone-faced, looking ahead, trying to pick up any shape on the River in the gathering gloom ahead.

'We must catch up with them soon,' she said. 'They can't possibly have made much headway on their own.'

Huy wondered what she was thinking. Perhaps she wanted to rescue her husband, make him see sense, avoid scandal. Perhaps it was that simple. Or perhaps she was not thinking at all. Just going through the motions for the sake of doing something. He wished there had been time to contact Aset.

Something bumped gently against the side of the boat and there was a swirl of red water behind them as they moved on.

'Crocodile,' muttered one of the sailors, looking at Huy. 'Don't worry. This boat's too big for 'em.'

'What if they've beached the boat, gone overland?' asked Taheb.

'Where would they go?'

'I wonder where they think they're going, anyway.'

Suddenly, in the midst of the darkness, they saw a darker shape, shimmering because it was still too far ahead for them to focus on it.

'Pull harder,' said Huy. The sailors rowed on. As they drew closer, they saw that the little boat ahead was bobbing, more violently than by any motion the current would have caused. At the same time, faint cries reached their ears.

The sailors, themselves looking in the direction the sounds were coming from, pulled the skiff around broadside to the current and held her there.

'What are you doing?' shouted Huy.

'Saving our lives,' the sailor who had spoken before replied evenly.

'You said we were too big to be in any danger from crocodiles.'

'Not when there are this many of them.'

Taheb tried to stand up and the skiff rocked wildly. 'Amotju!' she cried in a voice of unfathomable anguish.

The current was pulling the little boat up ahead further away from them. Around it, the water had begun to seethe. They could just see the two people on board stabbing out with their oars. Then the last glimmer of light drained from the sky and the wind carried their voices to the skiff no more.

It was accounted a death of high honour to be lost on the River, and as their bodies were not recovered, effigies of Amotju and Mutnefert were commissioned to be the hosts of their *Kas* in their tombs. The statue of Amotju was placed in his father's tomb, behind the great cedar doors; Mutnefert's was erected in the vault of her husband, which was not in the Valley, but in the burial place of the Northern Capital. Taheb managed her husband's obsequies with a frozen dignity, never again betraying by so much as the flicker of an eyelash the torment she had revealed in that one cry of her husband's name.

As for Huy, his work, such as it was, was done. There was nothing to report, no file to be closed, no gain to be had. Somehow time had closed over the whole business like river water over a stone thrown in. The hardest job was telling Aset. Her grief, though it was as intense as Taheb's was icy, excluded him from it no less. He wondered whether, after all, there was any mystery in Amotju's love for Mutnefert.

He returned to his small house in the city. It seemed dark and mean, and full of ghosts: Amotju, Rekhmire, Ani; but also Aahmes and little Heby, whom he longed to see so much that he could all but feel the strength of his little body in his arms. The days passed. The priests set about the task of removing the name of the old king from every monument and column with renewed vigour. The Medjays managed, by extending their patrols, to reduce the number of tomb robberies in the Valley. The sun shone and the River flowed.

Huy settled to the task of getting on with the rest of his life.